1

SECRET MARRIAGES

EDWARD IV, ELEANOR & ELIZABETH

BY J.P. REEDMAN

COVER BY C.K. DESIGNS

DEDICATED TO THE MEMORY OF JOHN ASHDOWN-HILL, WHO BELIEVED IN ELEANOR.

Prologue:
    Blore Heath

Winds crept across Blore Heath, cooling the heat of the September afternoon. It was the Feast of St Thecla, that follower of Saint Paul who had escaped martyrdom in a pit of wild beasts to become a patron of chastity, but no one on the Heath dwelt on martyred virgins or saintly ways, but instead prayed to God for their own safety in the hours that followed. Many offered up the bargain, 'Let me live and I'll be a good man'—if they did, they most likely wouldn't change, but such were the minds of men in the face of bloody battle.

Behind a thorny hedge, wild with unshorn branches, soldiers loyal to the House of Lancaster, lay in wait, their banners stirred fitfully by a wind that still held the warmth of passing summer.

Under the command of Lord Audley and Lord Dudley, they waited impatiently in the lee of that great hedge, watching its long shadows stretch and change as the sun moved over the lonely stretch of unkempt heath. Waited for their enemies, the followers of the House of York, who they were told were marching from the northern stronghold of Middleham Castle fronted by the powerful Richard Neville, Earl of Salisbury, who was hurrying to rendezvous with his kinsman, Richard Duke of York, at Ludlow in the Marches. The Lancastrian generals hoped Salisbury's haste would make him careless and inattentive—and then they could strike, keeping the Yorkists from joining forces and, hopefully, bringing down the great amongst them.

In the midst of the crowd of soldiers, some whistling, some half in harness, some sitting on the ground watching the sun play off breastplates, plumed helmets and gauntlets, Sir Thomas Boteler, the son of Sir Ralph Boteler, Lord of Sudeley, waited in silence. He had only fought once before, at St Alban's, and the heath was a world away from the deep gutters and timber-framed houses where a deadly game of cat-and-mouse had played out. Here, he was struck by the strangeness of the day—the haze in the air, the vivid colours of the sky, the smell of the earth beneath his feet, the muted hue of the vegetation covering the summer-withered expanse. Everything seemed unnaturally clear, strangely wonderful, and so dear, even the inconsequential—the hedge, the distant brook, the grass beneath his metal-shod feet...but by moonrise tonight, unless Salisbury got word of the Lancastrian presence and retreated, blood would be spilt upon that green grass, that fresh-smelling earth. Beauty would become a horror.

Turning his head, heavy with his metal helm, he squinted toward the stocky church tower at Mucklestone. A rumour had gone through the troops that the Queen, Margaret of Anjou, had ridden from lodgings at the Bishop of Lichfield's palace to watch the armies collide from the safety of Mucklestone's tower. To watch her loyal forces gain victory. For it *would* be a Lancastrian victory, none had any doubt—the soldiers of King Henry outnumbered those of the Earl of Salisbury by two to one. The Yorkists would be crushed utterly, sheep to be slaughtered.

Thomas sighed, fingering the hilt of the sword girt at his side—a family heirloom gifted him by his father, Ralph. His family were solidly for Lancaster, his sire having served Henry V in his glorious French campaigns and then Henry VI in the capacity of Lord High Treasurer of England. Ralph had once aggravated the younger Henry by crenellating his castle of Sudeley without the necessary permissions—but the King was of forgiving nature and soon pardoned him without any lasting ill-feeling. Probably because, plagued with madness, the King did not remember...

I must be bold like my father. Thomas tried to shore up his darkening mood by musing on glories of his sire's distant past. *Think of all the campaigns he fought in France, fierce and bloody. Yet he returned, victorious. I shall return too, on the morrow, when all this fighting is done…*

"You look thoughtful, my friend."

Thomas broke out of his reverie. Glancing over, he saw Sir Hugh Venables, Baron Kinderton, his armour gleaming dully in the muted sunlight. Sir Hugh was a Cheshire nobleman of similar age to Thomas.

"There is much to think on, when one waits for war, my lord."

"Indeed, the mind is always far too busy at these times," grinned Venables. His visor up, he drank from a long-necked flask handed him by his squire. "I do not think we will have long to wait now—and unless some terrible misfortune befalls us, Salisbury's men will fall into our trap. Their view of our forces will be blocked by the hedge. They will not see us and march blindly to doom."

"As long as no defectors tell them we are here," replied Thomas Boteler, gloomily.

"Who would show such treachery?" Hugh scratched his unshaven chin. "Ah, well, there was one of note who might have proved slippery, but he already deserted his rightful King before the march and joined York's men. It caused tongues to wag in the royal tent, I tell you; this man was no shiftless foot soldier but a knight of repute. And now off ILL repute!" He chuckled at his own joke; the squire, a carrot-topped lad smiled and nodded.

"And his name?" Boteler stared at the other man in surprise. He knew such calumnies frequently occurred, but it made his frayed nerves sharper to think of desertion and turncoats within the Lancastrian ranks. He wanted men to cover his back—not thrust a dagger into it.

"William Stanley of Holt."

Boteler whistled. The Stanleys were a powerful Lancashire family with large personal armies. "If William has proved false—what of his brother Thomas? Those two usually go about together as if they were twins born of one birth. Or so I've heard."

Venables made a face, his disgust clear. "He's wandering about with a few thousand well-armed men in his train, according to the scouts."

"But not on the field with my lords Audley and Dudley. Not with us."

"No. It seems Lord Stanley has been *delayed*. He swears his loyalty to King Henry, though."

"But you do not trust him. I can tell. Your expression darkens when you speak his name."

"No, I do not particularly trust the man, but I believe he will throw in his lot with us in the end. He is no fool, that one. He is merely keeping his *options* open."

"I'd call that treachery," said Thomas Boteler. "A man should declare for or against, not slither around like some serpent. It is…is dishonourable."

"Even if Lord Stanley did desert to join his brother, the King himself is not far away—he may be as close as Stafford with his forces. Humphrey Duke of Buckingham leads the Royal Army and he is an experienced commander. Look, Boteler, we cannot lose, Lord Stanley or no…"

Thomas Boteler crossed himself. "God willing."

"Aye. God willing. God and a trusty sword arm." He beckoned to his squire. "Boy, more drink. For me, and for Sir Thomas."

Hours crept on; time began to drag and heightened tension gripped the Lancastrian army hiding in the shadow of the great, tangled hedge on Blore Heath. Thomas Boteler's thoughts drifted from battle strategies back to his family. The old man, Ralph—truth be told, he had never got along particularly well with his father and never held any high positions within the King's government, which he thought might come his way because of his sire's high status at Court. Ralph Sudeley seemed to prefer the company of Thomas' older half-brothers, born to his mother Elizabeth Norbury during her first marriage to John Hende, a one-time mayor of London. John the Elder and John the Younger. Thomas rolled his eyes just thinking of his two dullard siblings with their identical names and identical sanctimonious manners. They had always acted as if they, a mayor's sons, were his equal, and were full of 'good advice' which grated on the ear— although Lord Sudeley seemed glad enough to hear it.

Therefore, although Sudeley Castle was fair to the eye, lying in its green valley with wooded hills that shone copper in Autumn rising around it, he preferred to stay on his own manor in Warwickshire. With Eleanor.

Eleanor. The hard lines of his face softened almost imperceptibly. Dark-tressed, gentle Eleanor with her rich doe- eyes and her great piety and intellect. His wife was of good stock, a daughter of the ancient and powerful Talbot family, descended from Edward I, the Despensers and the de Clares. Her sire, John, Earl of Shrewsbury was a renowned military leader called 'the Terror of the French,' who had fought at the Siege of Orléans and the Battle of Patay.

"We could use the likes of John Talbot here today," Thomas murmured, glancing over at the mustered Lancastrians, who were stirring fitfully and peering up at the sky, worried that the day was passing and there was still no sign of the enemy. No such possibility of a hero to rally flagging heart, however. The old Earl of Shrewsbury was several years dead, his heart buried in the doorway of St Alkmund's in Whitchurch. He had fallen at Castillon, taking England's hopes of maintaining its French possessions with him to the grave; a battle-axe had struck his skull, leaving him so disfigured his physician only identified him by a missing tooth. Eleanor had spent little time with her father, meeting him for the first time at the age of six due to his numerous campaigns abroad…and yet, she remembered him fondly. His two wives, Maud Neville and then the determined Margaret Beauchamp, Eleanor's mother, seemed fond of him too—despite his absences, he managed to father eleven children between the two women

Thomas scowled, thinking of the old Earl's handsome and sizeable brood. It was the one downside of his marriage to Eleanor—no children, despite having no lengthy separations as an impediment. Eleanor prayed daily to Saint Anne, asking her to intercede and end her infertility; a dispensation to eat meat on forbidden days was obtained in case her blood was weak, and they had even made a joint pilgrimage to the Shrine of St Thomas Cantilupe at Hereford, but despite their best efforts (which were more than passing pleasurable) there was no sign of a child. Eleanor's barrenness made him feel his position with Lord Sudeley was even more precarious; he'd hoped a healthy heir would bring him closer to the old man.

A strident shout brought his thoughts to a close; alongside him, the great army was stirring. A shining ripple of metal, men hastened to take their positions. Horses stomped and pikes clattered as the pike-men gathered in formation.

A few feet away, Baron Venables closed his visor with a loud snap. His voice came from deep within the shining helmet, its timbre made strange and surreal by the encasing metal—"Arise, my friend! Our foes have arrived at long last. Let us end this unpleasant matter. We will all feast together by nightfall—a celebration of victory and good cheer!"

Across the field, there was some hesitation amidst the front ranks. Banners had not yet advanced. A dust-stained scout galloped up the field, keeping against the walls of the hedge. "Salisbury," he gasped to the captains. "He's circling… he's put his wains in a circle. He knows we're here!"

"Christ," murmured Venables, on foot beside Thomas. "Bad luck. Well, Tom Sudeley, our feasting may have to wait a few hours."

"Bad luck, indeed," murmured Thomas, as he felt an uncomfortable nervous cramp in his guts. He did not want to admit any fear, but it was there, a serpent chewing at his bowels, turning them to water. He hoped he would not disgrace himself.

"*Forward*!" He jumped as he heard John Sutton, Baron Dudley, bark the order to advance in a booming, thunderous voice. Down the field Thomas marched, the soft, tufted earth breaking beneath his feet, his sword drawn and ready in his gauntleted hand. Around him from all sides, trumpets began to shout their challenges to the smaller army of Yorkists waiting beyond the waters of Wemberton Brook.

A thin flurry of arrows met their initial advance; the Lancastrians, undeterred, with confidence in their greater numbers, trudged onwards, a heaving sea of spears and pikes, revealing their massed splendour to their foes.

As their opponents came into clear view, the Yorkist army appeared to give ground, its archers sending one last volley of arrows over the waters of the brook, arrows that fell harmlessly into the great hedge. The foot soldiers recoiled a few steps, then a few more.

"Jesu, they are cowards!" Hugh Venables laughed. "They already know they are done and are in retreat! Fools! We will run them to the ground like hares; Queen Margaret says she wants Salisbury brought to her alive…or dead."

Another commotion to the right drew the attention of both Thomas Boteler and his companion Venables. Lord Audley was summoning a party of mounted knights in his contingent to his side. With a sharp blare of horns, banners streaming out against the sky, the horsemen plunged through the murk of Wemberton brook toward the retreating Yorkists.

Thomas's foot division stormed after the cavalry, shouting and roaring. On the wings of their division, artillery fired—not many cannons of gonnes had been brought to the field by either side, but enough to fill the skies with smoke and blast the ears with thunder.

Victory did not seem far away, a brief but decisive skirmish, then the foe overwhelmed while fleeing…but suddenly the unexpected happened.

The Yorkists retreat…*was not.*

Serpent-like, sinuous, the line of Salisbury's foot soldiers twisted, turned, consolidated their position on the heath. They were now facing the oncoming cavalry charge with pikes and halberds lowered and ready, a dense line of bristling steel. A line of death.

The first row of horsemen crashed into the halberdiers. A horse went down, legs flailing in the air, blood fountaining from a lethal wound in the belly. Other soldiers marched stalwartly forward, attempting to ring the horsed knights and then cut them down.

"Back! Back!" Lord Audley rose in his stirrups and shouted at the top of his lungs. "It's a trap!"

The knights wheeled their mounts—those who had not already been hemmed in by the surge of Yorkist foot soldiers. By now Thomas was knee-deep in the freezing waters of the brook, his sword clutched in his hand. Within the confines of his helmet, his eyes widened as he saw the armoured horses thundering back in his direction—with soldiers in the red and black colours of the Earl of Salisbury slashing at their heels.

A huge destrier thundered past him, almost knocking him off his feet into the water. He struggled to gain purchase, knowing a fall amidst the milling sea of men, especially while in the stream, could prove fatal.

Richard Neville's men were now on the streambank, engaged with both the riders and pike-men fighting for King Henry. A soldier lurched towards Thomas, wielding an axe; he shied aside, stumbling as the strong current struck his knees, making his steps slow and unsteady no matter how he tried to right himself. The axeman swung again; anticipating the blow, Thomas leapt aside in a haze of spray and the axe struck water that was already turning a ghastly shade of red. Gasping, Boteler charged forward and stabbed wildly at his opponent. He hit the man's broad breastplate with a clang; the soldier wavered for a second, then rushed at him again, unharmed.

All chaos had now broken loose with both sides fighting hand-to-hand in the stream and on the muddy, trampled banks. Bodies were falling; despite his restricted vision, Thomas saw the banner of Lord Audley, ermine with a *chevron gules*, shake and waver as his standard-bearer was surrounded.

He pushed through the heavy press of bodies in Audley's direction, but in the next moment, a horse, its rider dragging on the reins to manoeuvre it in the fray, struck him heavily from behind with a mace.

He plunged face-forward into the churning, blood-tinged waves of Wemberton brook. Water filled his helmet; he started to choke as he thrashed madly in mud and gore. He had dropped his sword amidst the water-weeds...*somewhere*...but the loss of one weapon was the least of his concerns...

He had to get up...*to breathe*...

His head broke the surface just as he managed to wrench off his helmet. Panting for air, he scrabbled around in the muck, trying to haul himself up amidst the heaving bodies. Water streamed down his face from his hair, obscuring his vision, near-blinding him.

Thomas saw an indistinct shape loom, blocking out the sun, and then a flash of light, a blade descending like a star fallen from the firmament.

And then, there was a bolt of white-hot pain, a ghastly scream.

His own scream.

His vision turned to red, a waterfall of blood.

And then...the darkness.

CHAPTER ONE

Eleanor Boteler stood within the chapel of the Manor of Fenny Compton. She had spent much time here since her husband Thomas rode out for war. On her knees she prayed that he be spared in the conflict—at the same time, she prayed for the souls of her father, killed at Castillon in 1453, her half-brother Christopher, murdered by a treacherous Welsh knight during a tourney, and her brother Louis, who had gone to his grave after a long and troubling illness the year before. She hoped she would not be adding one more name to that unhappy list.

Thomas will come back, she told herself, head bowed, her rosary of coloured glass, a Spanish import, clutched in her hands. *All will be made peaceful in the land by the actions of his Grace the King's army. He will come back and I will bear him a son...*

Her hand drifted down to her flat belly. She could not understand why God had not yet granted her and Thomas a child. Nearly ten years had gone by since they had begun to dwell as true man and wife, and in all that time there had not been a solitary time she had thought she might be pregnant. It was so strange; her mother had borne many children. Yet that was the last of her worries now. She wanted her husband home, alive and well.

She sank down on her knees before the altar, cool granite, the Rood rearing behind illuminated by light filtering through the tiny, round-headed windows. The day was unseasonably warm for September, a golden day, and as ever on hot days, the painted, plastered walls of the chapel, cool and thick as those of a castle, sweated. Little trails of moisture, like a line of tears, trickled over the face of a wall-painting of the Madonna high above.

Eleanor closed her eyes. She seldom dreamt but the night before last, with the bedclothes rucked up around her thighs and a thread of cool night-wind whistling through a crack in the shutters to soothe her over-warm flesh, she had a dream-vision of an angel, or at least what she supposed was an angel. A Saint Michael figure, wreathed in a radiant sunburst, holding up a flaming sword that was both symbol and challenge. A portent of the battle her Thomas found himself in? The angel's face had been beautiful but terrible and Eleanor had found herself waking, sweat-drenched, crying out. Her attendant, Agnes, had come stumbling toward her with a candle, her grey-speckled braids glittering in the feeble light and sleep-hazy eyes deep with worry. "What is it, Lady Eleanor? What ails you?"

Eleanor, gathering a rose-coloured robe, had brushed the maid aside and fled to the window where she threw open the shutters and gasped in the sharp night-air, her unbound locks streaming forward in a raven torrent. Deep, gasping breaths tore from her lips as she savoured the cold, clean scent of early morning and the hopeful glow of the first hint of dawn.

"My Lady?" Agnes squeaked at her back. "Are you ill?"

"It was just a bad dream, Agnes," she said at length, stepping back from the window pane and twisting her long hair into a braid. "Go back to bed, I bid you."

Agnes had slammed the shutters with a clatter. "Lady, the night air might strike you with a chill unto death. And what if someone had seen you in unseemly dress and with your head uncovered?"

Eleanor had laughed wryly, folding her arms. "Who would see me before dawn? A passing fox? I am sure old Reynard, sly and wily, would be truly shocked!"

Both women had laughed then and headed back to their rest, Agnes tucking her mistress under the counterpane with care. Their laughter on that strange, portentous morn had swiftly dispersed the memories of Eleanor's dream but now, here in the chapel, alone with her thoughts, alone in God's presence, she was reminded of it again.

Fragments of ancient stained glass still lingered in the narrow window-slit on the north side of the nave—images of angels weighing souls before God's Throne. Sunlight shone through the yellow panes that made up the angels' hair and sent patterns playing over the scrubbed flagstones.

Tearing her gaze away, she tried to quell the memories of dreams and portents and concentrate on her morning prayers. Never had her thoughts been so troubled, her mind so distracted…Well, it was to be expected; never had her husband left her side to fight for his King before. She knew such worry was the lot of a noblewoman in these troubled times, yet still she feared, and pious although she was, she could not quite trust God enough to believe he would bring her husband Thomas home unscathed. After all, he had not heeded her prayers for her father at Castillon either.

Instead of the Almighty Father, she decided to murmur a prayer to the Mother of Christ, the Blessed Virgin Mary. A woman who suffered much, who lost her only Son—surely, she would understand Eleanor's fears?

"Upon my side I me lay;
Blessed Lady, to thee I pray:
For the tears that you weep
Upon your sweet son's feet,
Send me grace for to sleep,
And good dreams for to meet
Sleeping, waking, till morrow day be.
Our Lord is the fruit, Our Lady the Tree,
Blessed be the blossom that sprang, Lady, of thee.
In nomine Patris et Filii et Spiritus sancti…."

A sound in the corridor beyond the back of the chapel made Eleanor jump. Was Agnes on some errand? She frowned. She had told her maid-servant she wished for seclusion while she was at her prayers.

Slowly, she rose from her knees and turned around. The chapel door was opening slowly. Sun spilt through the gap, cast a sword-like beam of light across the time-eroded tiles. She was dazzled for a moment, raising her hand to tearing eyes. Faintly she saw a man's shape silhouetted against the streaming golden light of that strange, hot September day.

For a moment, she thought, *Is it Thomas; is he home?*

The burst of light faded as the figure took a tentative step in her direction and closed the door. Now she saw that the intruder was her chaplain, Father Gray. His face was white, his hands knotted in his cassock. "Lady Eleanor?"

"Father Gray, what is it?" A needle of fear was darting in her breast, making her breaths shallow and ragged. Yet she must not be foolish and allow herself panic. It could be anything. A fire, a flood, a lost child in the village

"A man has come to the gate…"

"Did you let him in? Who is he?"

"He has ridden from a place called Blore Heath…"

"I do not know it." Frowning, she shook her head.

Father Gray took a deep breath. "A battle was fought there two days ago, my Lady. The man, a servant of Lord Sudeley, has ridden like the wind. With news." He stared down at the tiles, hands working nervously.

"What is this news?" Eleanor's voice emerged a harsh whisper. The blood beat in her head, a steady drum.

"The Earl of Salisbury won a great victory over Lord Audley. Audley is dead. Lord Dudley is captured. Many knights were slain, others gravely injured…"

"And Thomas, what of Thomas. Is he injured?" Eleanor grasped at any hope.

Father Gray's mouth worked but no words would emerge. He shook his head ever so slightly and crossed himself with a shaking hand.

Eleanor whirled away from the priest, grief and shock overwhelming her. She fell in a faint before the altar, with the bright angels weighing souls upon the Scales of Justice rising above her, the golden beams shooting through their locks colouring the pallor of her stricken face.

February. England was still cold but winter was losing its grip. Snow had ceased to fall and the roads had become passable in most places. With a small company riding alongside her chariot for protection, Eleanor Boteler fared from Great Dorset to Sudeley Castle, home of her father and mother-in-law.

Passing through the village of Winchcombe outside the castle gates, she heard the bells chiming in the great Abbey that stood amidst the small houses of timber and golden stone. Once upon a time, those bells had been happy sounds, when she was a young girl living under Lady Elizabeth's care, waiting to marry Thomas when she came of age. Now they sounded dreary and surreal, mourning bells tolling for a husband lost.

Pushing aside the curtain in her chariot, she peered out at the tall tower of St Peter's church, richly endowed in years past by Lord Sudeley. He had ordered the building decorated with gargoyles, each one a caricature of someone he knew, his wife, the church architect, choristers—and even Thomas. Fierce-visaged, dressed as a soldier with an expensive sword close to hand, Thomas's stony grotesque gazed with impassive blank eyes towards the distant towers of his ancestral home.

The home he did not live to inherit, the home no son of his body would ever own.

Eleanor dropped the velvet curtain, stared down at her hands as emotion roiled within her.

The carriage trundled on, past the gate-wardens and up through bare and clawing trees toward Sudeley Castle's tallest tower, where the wan February sun was peering like a baleful eye through a thin bank of dark-hued clouds.

"Eleanor, my dearest, I am so glad to see you." In the Great Hall, hung with rich Arras and decorated with armorial shields, Lady Elizabeth greeted the younger woman, kissing her warmly on both cheeks. "I wish the occasion was happier."

Eleanor gazed at Lady Elizabeth noting how she had grown suddenly old, her round cheeks sunken with grief. "So do I. I did not expect to be a widow so young…"

Lady Elizabeth sighed. "Yes, and a mother should not outlive her son. But at least I have two other sons…which is not to denigrate Thomas's memory," she added hastily. "But my husband, he…he is truly wretched for all that he puts on a brave countenance to the world. He now has no heir."

Eleanor blinked away tears. "I fear that is my fault, for I gave Thomas no sons."

"The fault was *war*, Eleanor." Elizabeth placed her hands comfortingly on her daughter-in-law's shoulders. "Now, come, I will take you to the gardens. Lord Sudeley awaits your presence there."

"In the gardens?" She was surprised he wished to meet there, for the air was still cold and no flowers or herbs yet grew from the slumbering earth.

Elizabeth nodded. "Yes, my dear, he has something to show you."

Eleanor left the keep and walked through the stubbly remains of the herb garden. Her breath hung ina cloud before her mouth; in the west, the sun was fading into a fog bank, casting a red glow over the undulating green landscape around Winchcombe—days were still short and nights all too long. In the east, a ghostly crescent moon was on the rise, riding a patch of flying cloud.

In the wake of Eleanor's approach, servants moved hurriedly to kindle torches and set them around the gardens for her use. Moths fluttered toward the orange flames, their wings white and ghostly, whirring as they battered against the castle walls, the stark fruit trees, the crown of Eleanor's tall headdress.

Up ahead, she saw the shadow of a building, faintly illuminated by the uncertain light. A stone chapel, half-completed. A figure leaning on a cane stood in the doorway.

Lord Sudeley.

Stepping up to him, she curtseyed. "Child, child, no need." He reached out and helped her to rise. "Come, kiss me, daughter."

She leaned over to kiss his cheek dutifully but also with real affection. Ralph Boteler was not much like Thomas in aspect, a short, burly man with grey whiskers and a red face that was normally cheerful but now had lost its smile. A scar marred one cheek, standing out white in the faint torchlight—an arrow had struck him while fighting for King Henry at St Alban's. Thomas had fought alongside his father then, and despite the filial bonds being not as strong as they might be, he had dragged his wounded sire to safety, while Edmund Beaufort was slain outside the Castle Inn and the Duke of Buckingham and the King injured.

"I am glad to see you, sir," she said, "but my heart is heavy at this meeting. My prior memories of Sudeley were wrought of gold, but now they have become rust upon the chill night of this sorrowful occasion." She glanced around; skeletons of dead flowers were pale ghosts in the beds. A leaf blown on the breeze brushed her cheek. "I...I almost expect him to be here still. Not dead...just hidden...."

Lord Sudeley sighed and hung his shaggy grey head. "He is at peace now, Eleanor. I transported his body to St Alban's where, I dare say, he saved my life long ago. It is a most beauteous Abbey, set about the shrine of a warrior saint, and I have masses said for his soul every day. Thomas...ah, Thomas. I miss him, Eleanor. I just wish we had not been so estranged. I never understood why we were; I think he pondered this truth also. We were like fire and water. We seldom saw eye to eye, even when we tried."

"He did love his father, though, I promise you," said Eleanor softly.

"Your words bring a small comfort to an old man. I am pleased we chose you for our son, Eleanor."

She gave him a wry smile, her hands folded modestly before her. "Truly, my lord? I should have given you grandchildren, as I told Lady Elizabeth."

"God does not grant us all things we wish, my dear," said Lord Sudeley with a sigh. His breath puffed out around his bearded lips, a ghostly cloud. "Look, ere all the light departs and the torches below. My beautiful chapel, in construction. Thomas will be remembered here; images of our friends and family shall adorn it in the form of grotesques. Maybe even you, my dear, although you could never be known as 'grotesque'. Myself now…"

"Oh, sir, how can you say such a thing?" blurted Eleanor. "You are not…"

Sir Ralph gave a sad little laugh. "I jest. And I see I have raised a smile on your face. So it should be. You will find joy in the future, my dear, I am certain of it. Marry again…"

She gasped as if in sudden pain and stared down at the grass, jewelled with dew.

"I know…it is too soon to talk of such events. So, let us talk of my chapel instead!" He gestured again to the half-built stone edifice behind him. "Above the west door, look—the first carved figures. You will recognise them at once, I dare say, his Grace King Henry and Queen Margaret."

Eleanor looked, squinting in the gloom. Behind Lord Sudeley on the arch over the door were indeed two stone heads—the passive King, his fierce, French-born Queen. Why did she feel a sense of dismay, even dislike? Where had King Henry been when Thomas was killed at Blore Heath? Wandering somewhere in the vicinity with the royal army. He saw no battle. And Margaret, who was said to have watched the fighting from atop the nearby church tower? She was said to have fled when the tide turned against her forces, compelling a local blacksmith to shoe her mount backwards so the tracks she left would confuse her enemies…

Eleanor forced such treacherous thoughts from her head. What did she expect, the Queen to ride down upon the foe like some legendary Amazon? Margaret was unrelenting and remorseless as she fought for the rights of her young son, Prince Edward, but she was not a fool. She would take charge of the King and her remaining troops and they would live to give battle another day...

"My dear Eleanor, are you well?" Lord Sudeley's voice floated through the shadows. "You look pale and strange."

"Just my imaginings, sir," she said in a low voice. "Silly things, passing fancies."

Hand on her arm, he gestured her inside the chapel. The roof was incomplete and the stars were hard diamonds in the blue-black sky above. There was no Rood or screen as yet, but the bare marble of the altar was vaguely luminous in the darkness.

"Shall we pray?" asked Ralph Boteler. "For Thomas? For a happier future?"

"Here?" she said in surprise. The torches were beginning to fail; the night-wind raked through the unfinished building, cold and uncompromising.

"Why not? With the roof unfinished, we gaze up at God's firmament unimpeded. How better to pray?"

"How better, indeed?" Another small smile tugged her lips.

In silence, they walked to where the altar rail would be raised and knelt side by side on the chill tiles. The stars wheeled overhead, turning toward dawn like the ever-changing Wheel of Fortune on which all men are bound.

Over the next few weeks, Eleanor engaged in business with Lord Sudeley, putting her mourning aside as best she could. Before she returned to Great Dorset, she had to deal with her lands. The manors given to her and Thomas were hers by dower rights but she decided to return Griff to her father-in-law, as a gift for his kindness. In gratitude, Ralph

Boteler issued a quitclaim on Fenny Compton which gave Eleanor complete rights over the manor. It was a fine property for a twenty-three-year-old widow to hold and would bring in sizeable rents.

"Now, my dear," said Lord Sudeley, when the deeds had been signed and sealed. "You know, of course, what I want from you in return for Fenny Compton."

Eleanor nodded. "Yes. As soon as I may, sir, I will endow Corpus Christi College in Cambridge—and you, Lady Elizabeth and my poor dear husband Thomas shall be remembered in prayers there for all time, along with deceased members of my own family."

Lord Sudeley took her by the shoulders and hugged her, which startled her. "Remember, you are still as a daughter to me and to Elizabeth. We shall pray for your future."

"I plan to visit my sister Countess Elizabeth at Framlingham as soon as I may," said Eleanor. "It has been too long since we sisters were together. I look to her for comfort."

"Yes, you must go and soon," said Lord Sudeley. "In family, consolation can be found."

Eleanor departed for the eastern counties in the company of Ralph Boteler's retainers which he kindly lent her to assure her safety, although England's troubles had subsided yet again. After the disaster at Blore Heath, the King's army had marched towards Ludlow, where the Duke of York had his stronghold, and although York readied to defend Ludford Bridge against the King, many of the Duke's men deserted at the sight of the Royal Banners, and York, his eldest sons and the Earl of Warwick fled abroad. No doubt they would return, but at present England was back in the hands of Harry Six.

Peering from her chariot, the young widow watched as the land grew flat, the skies wide open, the trees sparser and bonier than those in heavily forested parts of Warwickshire or the leafy green hills near Sudeley Castle.

At length she reached the little town of Framlingham, its timbered houses clustered about a neat grey church. Beyond stood the castle with its thirteen great mural towers strung out along the skyline. Her sister who dwelt there was a great lady, already the Countess of Surrey despite her youthful age—one day her husband would be Duke of Norfolk and she a Duchess. But at the moment Eleanor had no care for Elizabeth's future position—she was just wanted comfort from a cherished and much-loved younger sister.

Once in the inner ward of the castle, a bevvy of attendants swarmed to assist her from the chariot. She glanced around. This castle was very different from Sudeley. Although a family home, Framlingham bore a more martial feel, as if ready to be fortified against invasion at any time, and indeed once long ago King John had besieged it. Now, however, modern brickwork dappled the older stone and pleasure gardens grew within the walls, filled with roseries, fruit trees and herbs.

"Eleanor!" She heard her sister's voice, glad and informal. Glancing aside, she saw Elizabeth approach from the direction of the garden, the veil of her butterfly headdress sailing in the wind, a gown of deep amber brocade billowing about her ankles. Bet had always been the beauty of the Talbot family beside whom all her sisters paled, with fine dark eyes the hue of chestnuts and smooth skin as soft as bleached silk.

The younger woman caught her sister's hand. "Eleanor, how glad am I that you have come. You must dine with me in the solar. You must eat more; you must not become ill with grief. I will see that the best delicacies are laid on your trencher tonight."

The two women went together to Elizabeth's solar, high in one of the towers, its wide windows looking out over the artificial mere and vast deer park beyond the castle walls. It was a fine room, as befitted Elizabeth's status, with a blue tiled floor and *mille fleur* tapestries adorning the wall. Elizabeth's stool was heaped in cushions and draped in golden-hued silk; two candelabras burned sweet, expensive, tallow candles and pomanders dangled from the beams to freshen the air.

Elizabeth called for sweetmeats and wine to be brought, then had her ladies remove her huge headdress and comb out her hair. Her tresses were long and dark, falling around her like a midnight cloak. Eleanor looked at her with a tiny frisson of envy—unworthy of her, she knew, but Bet was extraordinarily beautiful as well as clever and accomplished, hence she had made the best marriage match of the family.

"I have spoken to John's father, the Duke" chattered Elizabeth. "He said you can stay with us for the rest of the year, even for Christmas, longer if you wish. I would be glad to have you stay at Framlingham. I…I…sometimes, it has been hard of late."

"Bet, what is wrong?" Eleanor leaned forward and caught up her sister's hands.

"It is my husband's father, Duke John. Illness plagues him—he is sick, he rallies—and my John is like a string pulled taut, ready to snap. I am afraid what will happen if he should die with John and I being so young."

"I am grieved to hear of his Grace's illness—are you sure you want another guest at this time?"

"Don't you *dare* think of leaving just yet, Nel. I need another woman's company and who better than one's sister? I have my own griefs too, which I can confide to none other."

"What griefs? John is kind to you, is he not?"

"Yes, but…we have no children as yet."

"Bet, you have only just begun to live together as man and wife. You are both very young and have years ahead of you. Now, if you had been wed ten years as I was with Thomas, and no child…it would be a different story." Suddenly Eleanor's face crumpled; tears began to fall.

Elizabeth placed a comforting hand on her shoulder and handed her a handkerchief. "We will have to get you married again, Eleanor…when the mourning period is over," she added hastily.

"I don't know if I wish to remarry. Maybe I shall retire to a religious life." Dabbing at her eyes, Eleanor gazed over at a small, exquisitely-carved alabaster crucifix fastened to the wall.

"Oh, don't say that! Eleanor, I would miss you so!"

Eleanor's lips quirked. "I did not say I'd become a cloistered nun! But to be truthful, I have not really thought much of the future. The past is still far too close."

"I understand," said Elizabeth. "Make no hard decisions right now, Nel. Think of the joyful days we will have together here at Framlingham. It will be like old times. Do you remember the things we got up to at our home at Blakemere? Mother thought we were the worst hoydens."

"I remember," Eleanor smiled. "We were wild, but mother really had nothing to complain about. At heart, we were good girls. If we were ever over-forward…well, maybe we just took after mother, hence she dared not complain! Remember the to-do she made over the Berkeley inheritance?"

Elizabeth nodded. "Yes, her cousin James ended up in the Tower after father spoke out against him. And then William Berkeley sent men to assail our tenants, and they took poor old blind Richard Andrews and set a hot brand to him." She shuddered at the memory.

"The poor man," murmured Eleanor. "I remember all too well."

"But that was the end for the Berkeleys!" Elizabeth said, suddenly full of family pride. "Their own man Rice handed over the keys to their castle and Cousin James and his four loutish boys were all captured in their beds."

"I hope we shall never again have such family entanglements."

"But the courts in Chipping Campden and Cirencester affirmed mother's *right* to the Berkeley lands. So much for

Isabel Mowbray, Lady Berkeley—when she made a claim against mother, she ended up in Gloucester prison."

"Where she died," said Eleanor in a low voice. "That was not a good thing, Elizabeth, to say nothing of the fact her death caused his Grace the King to confiscate *all* the involved lands. So, all the fighting—and death—was for nought."

Elizabeth stared into her lap, looking suitably chastened. "Yes…yes, of course it was wrong. Unseemly. Lady Berkeley was my husband's aunt, after all. I must be more circumspect in what I say, having married a Mowbray."

"Well, such a strong union will doubtless bring lasting peace between our families." Eleanor took on the tone of a lecturing older sister. "That's what we need, Bet. Peace. I pray I am never caught up in any scandals like our mother."

"Not even if they were *love* scandals?" Elizabeth teased, becoming what she was, in truth—a girl of sixteen summers. "And not battles over lands and money?

"Not even then!" said Eleanor with firmness. "I swear I will pray to God Almighty that I am not ever tempted to engage in such folly."

CHAPTER TWO

Newly returned from exile in Calais, Edward of March sat on his horse by the Headless Cross at Hardingstone just outside the town of Northampton. Over his head soared the graceful arches of the octagonal cross, a memorial to Eleanor of Castile, the wife of King Edward I, marking where her body rested on its journey to Westminster Abbey in London. At the young lord's side rode Richard Neville, Earl of Warwick, and Cardinal Thomas Bourchier, Archbishop of Canterbury.

The Archbishop was speaking in angry tones, "They refuse to treat with us, my lords. The Duke of Buckingham would not even let us near the King's tent."

"So it was with my heralds—they were turned away with curses and threats," said Warwick darkly, rubbing his chin. "We have no choice now but to attempt the assault, whether the Royal Standard flies or not. We outnumber the bastards, after all."

Edward, unhelmed, his hair lank and dark in the light rain falling from the heavens, peered through the fringe of trees bordering the deer park of De la Pre nunnery. Through the murk, he could see the arches of the priory, the square block of its church, and beyond it in the far distance, the faint parapets of Sandyford Bridge and the red-stone bulk of the town's Lazar House. Between convent and bridge, with their backs firmly to the river, King Henry's army lurked behind a series of newly-dug trenches and embankments.

"They have entrenched themselves well." Edward's voice was calm. "They seek to set up artillery in the manner it is done in France."

"Aye." Warwick fiddled with his horse's reins as he stared hawkishly over the fields toward the enemy. "Sir John Talbot the Younger is one of the commanders; he fought with his father at Castillon…"

"Where his father was killed," said Edward wryly.

"Aye."

"Maybe history will repeat itself." Edward's mouth curved into a less than friendly smile. "Now, let us head for the town and meet the rest of our forces! It is my intent to make the folk of Northampton pay for their support of Lancaster, in the same way that Ludlow suffered because of its support for my father's rightful cause!"

Wheeling his mount around, Edward applied his spurs and galloped down the road towards the walled town in the far distance. Warwick and the Archbishop rode hard on his heels, mud flying up from beneath their horses' hooves.

"The young Earl of March is keen indeed," panted Bourchier to Warwick as trees, bushes and cottages flashed by.

"Edward is eager for battle." Warwick 's voice held a hint of pride—Edward was his protégée, they had fled together to Calais after the disaster at Ludford Bridge, "and also to rendezvous with Lord Scrope and Sir John Stafford. He wants to be certain of their loyalty and commitment."

Suddenly there was a movement in the trees on the right-hand side of the road. Warwick shouted an alarm, and Edward yanked his mount around just as a hail of arrows descended upon him and his men. "Attack, we are under attack!" shouted Warwick as the foliage parted and a horde of swift-moving soldiers with spears and pikes began to harry the flank of his contingent.

The Yorkist forces turned to meet their oncoming foes, as rain began to fall in torrents from the sky, driving into men's faces and hindering visibility; it was hard to tell who was friend and who was foe. A strong wind screamed down the London Road and set the trees dancing.

"It is Lord Beaumont!" Warwick's men cried, pointing to a banner that abruptly opened amidst the Lancastrians—a lion rampant on an azure field full of Fleur de Lys.

Warwick bridled with red-hot anger as he saw the banner flap mockingly through the downpour; Beaumont was wed to his aunt Katherine which made the attack somehow rankle even more. Teeth gritted in grim defiance, he signalled for his division to march forward and meet the assault head-on.

The skirmish on the roadside did not last long. Warwick's men, wearing their Ragged Staff badges, managed to push Beaumont's forces back into the shadows of the trees, and with the rain driving into their faces and hampering visibility, they soon fled for the safety of the hastily-thrown up earthen ramparts near the nunnery, St Mary de la Pre.

Edward and Warwick watched them go, holding back from chasing after them. When they were out of sight, dim blobs in the rainy distance, Edward gave the order to continue onwards and the Yorkist army marched at speed towards Northampton.

When they arrived, the commanders were pleased to find the bridge intact, the waters from recent rains swirling between its tall arches. Any guards on the parapets had long since fled.

Over the bridge the Yorkists marched, iron-shod feet clashing on the damp stonework, as they entered the lower part of Northampton near the Hospital of St John. Stern and unbreached, the town walls, became visible ahead through the dank murk. Further on, guarding the hill that led into the town centre was a great towered gateway. The gate was closed, barred against them by the fearful townsfolk. As the army approached a handful of defenders appeared on the turrets and half-heartedly hurled a few missiles in their direction.

Edward made a signal and his archers fired at the shapes half-concealed by the rows of crenels above. The heads of the defenders bobbed; vanished.

"The door is of inferior quality." Richard Neville, Earl of Warwick, eyed the wooden gate stretched between the vast bulk of the two gate-towers. Made from mighty oak, time had whittled its strength away; wormholes threaded through it. "Break it down."

A section of his men broke away and began attacking the door. They had no ram, for sieges were rare in these times, but it turned out no ram was necessary. Using axes and picks the soldiers smashed their way through the dry wood, ripping the door asunder before tearing it from rusty hinges. Men poured into the breach, shouting triumphantly as they lifted the great wooden bar on the far side to allow the mounted commanders to enter Northampton unimpeded.

The streets beyond were empty, the vast market square around the church of All Saints as desolate as if a plague had carried the town's inhabitants away. A few rats scurried amidst the detritus found in every town.

Warwick glanced over at Edward; the young leader had lifted his visor and was surveying the scene before him—the desolate streets, the barricaded Guildhall, the closed Greyfriars priory. He raised an arm for attention and a long sigh rippled through the men gathered at his back. "Do as you will."

The soldiers surged around him on his steed and raced across the expanse of the market square. Doors were pummelled and kicked open in Draper's Row and Silver Street; screams sounded as the Yorkists dragged out the townsfolk hiding inside. Someone stuck a torch into an abandoned wain brimming with baled hay; flames and smoke leapt into the air.

"Is this wise?" Warwick eyed Edward.

"Wise? Maybe, maybe not. What it is, Dick, is retribution for Ludlow. It will…" he grinned, his white teeth flashing in his ardent young face, "punish those who help our foes. It will also give our 'friends' in the fields below the chance to see that no quarter will be given when we join them in battle."

Smoke began to curl up from the roofs of buildings in Northampton town, from the merchants' shops around market down Gold Street to Mare Fair, the churches of St Peter and St Gregory and the closed gates of the semi-ruinous Royal Castle.

Edward continued to watch, while Richard Neville went to meet the incoming forces of their allies, Scrope and Stafford, who had entered through Derngate.

"It is time." At length, Warwick rode up on his grey and beckoned to his protégé "We must call these dogs off and set to the business of war. Scrope and Stafford are ready to fight and are firm for our cause; our forces are complete."

"Then let it be so. I am ready." Edward pulled down his visor with a clang. Atop his destrier, he looked like a giant, towering far above all other men within the ranks.

Warwick, the more experienced in warfare, with years of fighting behind him, raised himself in his stirrups to address the gathered host assembled around the market square and adjacent streets. "The time is now!" he roared, waving his sword aloft in gauntleted hand. "God is with us against those who unlawfully pervert the rule of England! Remember that, men. And I bid you harken to me...look to the *Ravestock Noue*, the Black Ragged Staff that is the badge of Lord Grey of Ruthin, and leave those that wear it unharmed. Grey has now declared for our cause; his levies will fight our enemies. I also bid you, in the name of all that's holy, not to lay violent hands on King Henry or on common folk who may serve him in his camp; strike in anger only at lords, knights and squires."

The Yorkist host began to filter out of the shattered Southgate, back over the bridge, past St John's and St Thomas's hospitals, past the Lazar House of St Leonard with its enclosed graveyard, and into the leafy deer park of St Mary's convent.

There, before the hastily-constructed ramparts of their foes, the Yorkists took positions, with Lord Fauconberg, a war-hardened, steely-eyed little man who was a kinsman to both Warwick and March, taking the left, Richard Neville as main combatant in the centre, and Edward, who was not yet tried in the field, on the right.

The young warrior, facing his first major battle, seemed as cool as if it were his hundredth. The banner of his father, the Duke of York, streamed out above his helmeted head, proclaiming his lineage and his right.

Then forth from the host came Francesco Coppini, the papal legate from Rome, and he flew the banner of the Church so that all men could see it, and in a great voice absolved the Yorkists of all their sins before the battle commenced.

Coppini then produced a parchment scroll and held it aloft so that both sides of the conflict could see it. In a deep, heavily-accented voice, he cried out, "Behold, I bear with me the means to excommunicate, to ban under Anathema the unrighteous from receiving the Holy Communion, from attending Mass, even from burial in Christian ground. Like Satan cast from heaven, those who fight against the true lords of England shall be cast into the pits of fire! Woe betide those who do not lay down their weapons."

A low, uneasy murmur rippled through the King's army behind the earthen defences; the harsh words were directed at them and what man did not fear the pits of fire? The common soldiers looked to each other nervously through the dismal sheets of pouring rain.

Proclamation delivered, Coppini retired to Warwick's side, thrusting the excommunication document for protection under his heavy cloak. "I have said what must be said," he muttered, swinging up onto his horse with the air of a squire. "Now I will join the Archbishop of Canterbury up at the Headless Cross to watch the battle proceed." Hurriedly he made the sign of the Cross over Warwick and Edward. "May God go with you, my lords. May our Saviour in His mercy and glory grant you victory today."

The papal legate and his followers departed in the direction of Hardingstone. Warwick waited in the rain as Edward returned to his wing on the right. Then the Earl had the trumpets blown and his own cannons fired, the latter to cause confusion and fear in the foe than to cause actual harm.

There was a brief return of fire, both a cannon and a few sputtering hand gonnes, but not as much as he had expected there might be; smoke hung for a second in the damp air then dispersed. The wet weather was taking its toll on any fire-power.

"Advance banners!" Warwick shouted to his men and, covered by the archers, the pikemen and foot soldiers began a slow, determined march towards the Lancastrian defences.

Beside him, clad in brilliant whyte armour that clashed with the leaden, weeping sky, young Edward of March, only eighteen summers old, Prince, Plantagenet and vengeful son, went to war for his father's cause.

CHAPTER THREE

"Bloody rain!" snarled John Talbot the Younger, Earl of Shrewsbury as the torrential downpour flooded the Lancastrian encampment. It was a bad omen, surely—the sky weeping over the entrenchments like a mourner might weep over a grave. The water had also deadened the Lancastrian cannons and the archers were scrambling to change bowstrings and shoot through eyes sluiced with water. Nevertheless, no army had ever been defeated, to the best of his knowledge, when situated behind earthen defences such as were raised on the field—not without days of assaults or destruction of the supply trains.

Talbot shook his head, clearing the rain from the eye-slits in his helmet. God, he wished he was anywhere but here in this muddy swamp! He thought of his wife Elizabeth and his seven children, the youngest only a few months old. He wished he was with them but knew his duty. His father, the first Earl of Shrewsbury, had been a hero in the French Wars; he must show similar mettle in the English ones. So far, he had not done particularly well; he had lost his position as Treasurer and his attempts to mediate the Loveday between Richard of York and Queen Margaret had failed. The rivals had held hands and processed through the crowds as intended but Margaret had glared daggers at York and the Duke looked no more enthused than she, holding her hand with clear revulsion as if it were a witch's mottled claw. Owing to his failure, the King had sent Talbot from court to become Chief Justice of Cheshire, but he'd continued trying to curry favour—indeed, he had been instrumental in getting parliament to bring a ban upon the Yorkists. With any luck, if he acquitted himself well here at Northampton, his troubles with King Henry might be, at last, over.

He grimaced, feeling rain slide under his armour, yet the hidden expression of disgust was for far more than the dankness. It was hard to accept that his youngest sister Elizabeth was wed to one of his enemy's supporters, and it did not help his cause with the King, but there was no helping it. He could only hope that his other sister Eleanor, widowed now, and as of her last letter residing temporarily in Framlingham, would not succumb to the blandishments of any Yorkist lord lurking around the Mowbrays. No, he was certain she would not—Eleanor would not betray her family, the legacy of her illustrious father. Nel was loyal, less flighty than Bet, and her husband had died at Blore Heath fighting the Yorkists besides. She would have no love of York's White Rose...

Talbot glanced over his shoulder; a few yards behind him King Henry's massive pavilion juddered in the wind, raindrops splashing off its brightly painted fabric. A door-flap was cast open and an old, slightly yellow and bleary-eyed faced peered out. "Where am I? What is happening? I heard the cannons fire—it startled me! Is it over? Where is Margaret? Where is my Queen?" Henry's voice rose in pitch as if he would suddenly start to scream.

The Duke of Buckingham, Humphrey Stafford, a grizzled warrior whose face was marred one side where an arrow had struck him at the Battle St Alban's, tried to calm the windswept monarch teetering in the opening of the tent, his mouth hanging and his eyes wild. "Your Grace, it will all be over soon. Be at peace, I beg you. You need not worry yourself. You can trust my word."

But Henry was hanging onto the tent flap, his bony fingers kneading the canvas. "Why do they attack me?" he whined plaintively. Rain trickled down deep furrows in his face, making him look as if he wept copious tears. "Why, Buckingham? Why does cousin York hate me so?"

"Your Grace, I beg you return to the safety of your pavilion. You are in danger here; you are not even in harness." Buckingham could not keep the exasperation from his voice as he tried to cajole the King back into the tent.

Suddenly there was shouting from the front of the great barricades. Instantly Earl John's attention was torn from the frustrated Duke and pathetic old monarch The Yorkists had crept up through the dimness and reached the earthen ramparts that the Lancastrians had raised. Launching a vicious assault, they tried to gain purchase on the muddy banks and scramble over the top into the camp. Pikemen struck at them, attempting to spear them as they climbed. Some fell wounded or dead into the ditch, but others managed to fight their way with axe and sword into the first ring of the defended enclosure.

Talbot drew his own sword, preparing to rush forward to assist his men. As he did, the wind screamed again and the rain, already a torrent, began to thunder down with almost supernatural force, blinding the embattled soldiers on the ramparts.

The drumming of the rain was almost like hooves...or *was* it truly hooves? Talbot whipped his head around in the direction of the noise. *Jesu!* Yorkist cavalry was riding furiously towards the right-hand section of the barricade. His lip curled in contempt. Fools! Grey of Ruthin was camped on that side with halberdiers, pikemen, and cannons—if any of the bloody things could still fire. The enemy would not get past Grey, speeding horses or no.

Within his helm, his eyes widened and a chill raced through his frame. But ...but the riders *were* over the hump of the ditch; he could see the banner of York rising, the Falcon clawing the rain-filled sky. Where in God's name was Grey of Ruthin?

A shout of alarm tore from his throat and he gestured wildly to his followers to engage. Edmund Lord Ruthin's men had laid down their weapons and parted like the Red Sea before the incoming enemy. The army of York was piling through the gap, fronted by a giant of a man in armour that glistened white-silver through the pounding rain.

In front of Talbot, another section of the fortification fell; men were clambering over tumbled earthworks; a hastily-constructed wooden palisade was ripped down. He saw the standard of Warwick loom, the Bear holding the Ragged Staff snarling evilly. Soldiers in red poured through a breach, weapons at the ready.

Hearing a shout for assistance at his back, he turned abruptly. It was Buckingham. A group of enemies had surrounded the Duke before the door of the King's pavilion. They pressed in with swords and pikes—a sea of glistening steel. "To me!" Stafford yelled desperately, parrying blows with his sword. "To the King! To the defence of the King!"

John Talbot hurried towards the beleaguered tent. In the perimeter of his vision, he saw Lord Egremont and Lord Beaumont also rushing to Buckingham's aid.

As he ran, a man loomed out of the milling confusion and struck at his head with a sword. The blade glanced aside on his well-made helmet, leaving his ears ringing from the force of the blow. He thrust the man away, then kicked him to the ground, dispatching him with his poniard.

The fighting had worsened around the King's pavilion. Buckingham was overwhelmed. With horror, Talbot watched as the old man's helm was ripped away and an axe smashed onto the top of his pate, shattering his skull. He fell and the attackers cheered to see his standard with its Swan and Cartwheels crash to the ground, the standard-bearer spitted on a blade and falling near his master.

Egremont went down next, slipping in the churned mud. Yorkist soldiers piled onto him, hacking and hewing. Beaumont held on slightly longer, trying to get his back to the royal pavilion, but a nearby archer shot him at close range, finding a chink within his armour. He crumpled without a sound and the hordes ran over him, taking furious vengeance upon his inert form.

Talbot was alone, fighting like a madman in a sea of crashing bodies. Blood spewed—not his own—running in shining rivulets down his plate armour. His heart beat loud as the Yorkist drums, which grew closer, ever closer, playing a death-tattoo amidst the blood and rain.

Suddenly a great shape loomed out of the murk, water and gore splashing over the broad shoulders, wide breastplate, ornate gauntlets. A battle-mace was raised, head gleaming, full of deadly intent. Behind the man, the wind fluttered the Falcon and Fetterlock standard of York and next to it, the White Lion of March.

Talbot tried to lunge forward, to remember all he had ever been taught of swordsmanship, but his opponent was *huge*, more intimidating than any enemy he'd ever fought in France. A great arm slashed down; Talbot cried out as his own arm was struck and jerked out at an odd angle, the bone between shoulder and elbow snapping like a twig in a flash of blinding pain.

For a moment he saw his opponent's eyes—the two men stood that close, almost breastplate to breastplate—through the slits in his visor; golden-green eyes, shining, hard as flints.

They held him as a serpent holds its prey fixed in its deadly gaze, and then came the pain, the thrust of uncounted blades all around, and falling down, down into the mud, he saw the banner bearing the great fierce Falcon, its curved beak open as if to feast on his ruined flesh, billow in victory against the dimming sky…

CHAPTER FOUR

Clad in soft velvet robes of mourning black, the two sisters Eleanor and Elizabeth sat in the solar of Framlingham Castle, trying to concentrate on their stitchery. "I cannot believe John is gone," said Elizabeth in a tremulous voice. Her needle shook in her hand. "His son and heir is but twelve years old, poor lad."

"It is this terrible war of cousins that afflicts our nation, Bet," said Eleanor sorrowfully. "I had hoped the Duke of York would never return to England after fleeing at Ludford Bridge. But he is back with his sons, and I fear things will get worse before they get better…"

Elizabeth wiped at damp eyes. "The Queen will never accept the Act of Accord that names York and his family heirs to the throne. Never. She is too proud and what woman would see her own child disinherited? She will battle York until one of them is dead."

Eleanor crossed herself. "What a terrible thought! To think, a woman pushed to such straits that she must act in the manner of a man."

"I have met the Queen several times," said Elizabeth. "I would not bat an eye if she should appear on the field of battle clad in armour!"

"Really?" Eleanor's dark eyes widened.

"No, I am only jesting!" Elizabeth grasped her sister's arm and cast her a wobbly smile. "Ah, we could all use some laughter—we have lived too long with misery and tears."

"Aye, that we have, Bet. But evil misfortune cannot surely last. We must pray that our burdens are soon lightened and the great and good sort out their differences—not by bloody battles but by cool deliberation."

Elizabeth nodded. "It would do well to have all ills sorted by…by Christmas." She sounded like a little girl, even younger than her sixteen years. "I am so looking forward to my first Christmas here with my husband!" She suddenly flushed, remembering Eleanor's recent bereavement. "Oh, Nel, forgive me…"

Eleanor touched Bet's shoulder reassuringly. "You meant no harm." It was good to see her sister's eyes brighten.

"You will stay, won't you, Nel? We'll be the most beautiful ladies in our new gowns! And once Advent is over, we will feast at the most marvellous table ever with peacocks and subtleties shaped like towers and lions! We'll dine like royalty all the way to Epiphany!"

"Yes, on sweetmeats, candied almonds and mince-meat tarts!" Eleanor was enjoying the thoughts herself now, thinking back to childhood celebrations with Bet at their father's manor of Blakemere.

"And *pommesmoile*—apple pies."

"What about a fat goose?"

"Of course! We could set up a nativity cave, as did the holy St Francis, filled with images of the Christ Child, the Blessed Virgin and the Magi."

"Yes, or we could dress like angels and sing a Yuletide song to praise Our Lady:

There is no Rose of such virtue
As is the Rose that bare Blessed Jhesu.
Alleluia.

For in this fair Rose contained
Was Heaven and Earth in little space,
Res miranda."

"What do I hear—the voices of angels?" Both women started in alarm as John, Duke of Norfolk, and Elizabeth's husband, John the younger, Earl of Surrey, entered the chamber unannounced.

Elizabeth's cheeks flamed rose-red "Your Grace! My Lord Husband! The visit is unexpected."

"We were merely passing and heard your voices, including Lady Eleanor's winsome song."

"I hope you are not angered," said Eleanor quickly, trying to hide her embarrassment. She had seen little of the

Duke since her arrival—though not an old man, he was crabbed and liverish of complexion; the castle cooks said he suffered bad dyspepsia no matter what he ate. Physicians went to and fro from his chambers day and night.

"Of course, I'm not, my dear!" Duke John smiled his crooked, pain-wracked smile. "It cheered me greatly. And it is true, soon Christmas will be upon us and we must celebrate as appropriate, including with the Lord of Misrule. After all, this year, we will have a guest."

"A guest? Who, your Grace?" asked Elizabeth, rising from her seat. "Not…not the King or Queen?"

"No," said the Duke. "Edward, Earl of March. He will be travelling in the east and it would please him to stop with loyal friends."

"Oh," Elizabeth breathed. She could find no words to say to her father-in-law. She saw her husband, sixteen-year-old John, eyeing her with some speculation. Young John's family were in the Yorkist camp and she knew this—she knew, too, that as a good wife, she must follow her husband's allegiances. But it was difficult when she thought of how March and Warwick had wrought her half-brother's doom at Northampton.

Eleanor put down her needlework and folded her hands to keep them from shaking. She did not need to entertain York or pretend she was pleased. "I think perhaps I should leave before that time. I would not wish to take a bed from the Earl and his entourage."

"Eleanor, no!" cried Elizabeth, catching at her sleeve, uncaring that the Duke and her husband were watching with surprise. "I want you to stay! Please reconsider!"

Eleanor shook her head and sighed. "No, my thoughts of staying were but idle fancies in truth. I must get hold of myself and face my future, for good or ill. My lands have been long unattended, left in the care of others while I travelled. I must take my duties to my tenants more seriously. I must go home."

The Duke of Norfolk took her hand and raised it to his dry, cracked lips. "If you will not stay longer, then may God go with you, Lady Eleanor. May you find peace and contentment in the days that are to come."

CHAPTER FIVE

Snow lay on the ground around the manor of Great Dorset. Eleanor walked across the courtyard, booted feet crunching on the frozen whiteness. The day was clear and bright, the sky blue, but the cold ate into the bones. Woodsmoke hung heavy in the still air; somewhere in the nearby village, a man was chopping kindling for the fire, his axe-blows making a rhythmic *crack, crack, crack*! Old Cook scurried across the yard, chasing a chicken that had fled its coop; she slipped on ice and landed on her large posterior, bringing a gust of laughter from the laundry woman swaggering along with her basket of linens on her hip.

"Don't you be laughing at me, Peg Pollock!" Cook screeched as she struggled to sit up and the errant chicken scuttled away. "It could be you next time and then you'd have to wash all those garments all over again!"

"Won't be me—I mind my step, I do" said Peg, nose in the air, and then, as if God on high had tired of the two women jibing at each other and sought to teach a lesson, Peg's foot hit a snow-hidden stone and head over heels she flew, the contents of her wicker basket sailing out onto a mucky patch of mud and sludge.

Cook gave a shrill cackle worthy of the evillest witch and pointed a pudgy finger at Peg. "Pride comes before a fall!" Peg began to splutter and wave her fists.

Fearful that the two old beldames would come to fisticuffs, Eleanor raced over to place herself firmly between them. "Cook, Peg, enough! What on earth are you two thinking of, fighting like a couple of trollops on the docks!"

"Ooh, milady!" Cook made a wobbly curtsey, showering mud off her apron and coarse woollen dress. "I didn't see you there. Forgive me."

"You are forgiven," said Eleanor with a sigh, "but both of you, attend to your work! The year has turned cold, we won't be able to do much washing before long. Nowhere to dry the linens, so let's not make additional work for ourselves, shall we? As for the chicken…" She turned and gazed toward the open gate leading from the courtyard toward the village. The chicken Cook had been chasing, affrighted by the squabbling women, was strutting about outside and like to vanish into the bushes that surrounded the manor. "Well, times are not as good as they once were. We cannot afford to lose any livestock, even a solitary old hen."

"Oh, milady, I'll go get that bird!" cried Cook, hoisting up her skirts and starting to run, or rather, waddle through the muddy courtyard. "I had no intentions of letting the ornery beast get away…till I was disturbed by those with nought better to do!" She cast Peg a malicious glare before stomping down toward the errant hen, who was pecking at the ground near the gate.

"I will help you, Cook," offered Eleanor. She was eager to do something to occupy her mind. Yes, the day to day running of the manor took time but she was weary of being on her own, of having no one to converse with save the servants. Perhaps she had been far too hasty in leaving Framlingham and her sister Bet…

At the manor gate, she made a half-hearted grab at the absconding chicken, who gave a great squawk and scuttled off into the bushes just as Eleanor had feared. "Oh, evil luck!" she cried. "If we don't coax her out of hiding, a passing fox will have a good meal tonight!"

"I'll be damned if I'll let that happen!" harrumphed Cook. "She's a good layer, that one. Too good to lose." The burly woman got down on her hands and knees, hem trailing in the muck, and started scrabbling in the bushes. There was a fluttering sound as the incorrigible bird vanished deeper into the tangle.

"It's useless, Cook," said Eleanor. "Don't worry about it. I will see if enough coin can be spared to get another laying hen from the market."

"Oh, it's all that Peg's fault, you should garnish the wench's pay," whined Cook, getting up and grimacing as her back made a loud crack. "She's bad news, no respect, you mark my…"

"Cook, hush, I bid you!" Eleanor stood still, staring in the directions of the village. The wintery glare was blinding, the sun falling in flames behind the spire of the church, and she shaded her eyes with a hand. Faintly he could hear the sound of hooves approaching at a rapid clip. A messenger? Who could be sending a letter to her? She almost dreaded any messengers now lest they brought evil tidings.

Through the brightness, the silhouette of a horse appeared, its rider upright and clad in a travellers' heavy mantle. A man of some means by the look of the horse and the fabric of the cloak. A small group of mounted companions trotted a few paces behind him.

"Who…who goes?" Eleanor asked, still struggling to see. "We are not expecting visitors here."

"No greetings for a kinsman?" asked a voice. She struggled to recognise it, shook her head.

"How soon you've forgotten. It's Tom. Thomas Montgomery!"

"Tom!" Eleanor stared in surprise. Tom was a cousin of her late husband. In the first years of her marriage to Thomas, Tom Montgomery had visited the manors of Griff and Great Dorset frequently, but when he had thrown in his lot with the Duke of York's party, tensions had arisen between him and Thomas and he came no more. She had not expected to see him again.

"What are you doing in these parts?" she asked, then blushed for she sounded both abrupt and rude.

"I am…*scouting* for a place where a great nobleman can stay the night. I thought of the manor of Great Dorset; it is out of the way, private."

"It is that!" said Eleanor, with a wry smile. "But it is not fitting for a 'great lord.' I am a widow woman now, Tom, and my circumstances are, alas, rather straitened. Lord Sudeley was more than kind in dealing with my property but I live with only a few servants and do as best I can."

"I understand your reluctance," said Tom Montgomery, "but this is a matter of some importance. Look, I have a letter here."

He thrust a gloved hand inside his doublet and pulled out a rolled parchment. He proffered it to Eleanor. She did not take it.

"Who is it from?" she asked.

"Your uncle, my lord the Earl of Warwick."

Her heart jumped. Warwick! His wife Anne Beauchamp was her mother's half-sister. She had met him once or twice, a proud man who brooked no fools, and who seemed tense as if he were a cannon about to explode. What could he possibly want with her?

"I have not seen my uncle of Warwick since I was a young maid," said Eleanor. "I fear I cannot see why he would desire contact after all this time."

"Just read his missive, I beg you," said Tom, with an appealing smile.

Hesitantly Eleanor took the parchment and unrolled it with some trepidation. Inside, her uncle by marriage spoke her fair and asked that she '*by God's Grace*' should put up '*a wanderer in need of shelter as the Christ Child and his Mother, the Holy Virgin...*" He also offered a considerable amount of money to pay for provisions—meat, poultry, beer, wine. Lots of wine. Eleanor's eyes widened. Even when Thomas was alive, they had never had such sumptuous stores as Warwick was offering.

"Uncle Warwick spoke fairly of the Christ Child," she said with cynicism, "but I have no doubt it is not He, nor his Blessed Mother faring to Great Dorset. Or the three Wisemen, for that matter."

"Nel, can you not guess who Warwick might send?"

"No, I cannot…and I grow cold out here. The sun has set."

"Will you do it? I must give Lord Warwick an answer as soon as possible."

Eleanor bit her lip. The sun had vanished in the west and blue twilight was falling. She noted Cook had gone very still and was no longer worrying about the fate of her favourite hen but rather listening in while pretending not to. The young noblewoman despised this cloak-and-dagger behaviour but the money and goods were tempting—and she had no wish to get on her uncle's bad side, either. "Oh…tell him yes," she blurted, "if it is so important!"

"It is," said Tom Montgomery. "I swear it."

"And will you be staying the night? You look half-frozen."

"No. I must carry your message to Lord Warwick at once. And Eleanor, be not fearful; I know you to be of great heart as well as great beauty …"

"But not great intellect," she said dryly, folding her arms, "since I am opening my home to Jesu knows what."

"You do yours wrong, Nel," he grinned, gathering up his reins. "So, it is farewell for now, but we will be back soon." He turned his horse's head; the beast snorted, the air before its nostrils a white cloud.

"When?" Eleanor clutched her own arms, barely able to control a sudden shivering that had gripped her. Was it the night's bitter coldness or something else? Some presentiment of future trouble?

"Four days, if all is well," Thomas Montgomery shouted over his shoulder as he rode back down toward the village of Great Dorset. "Be prepared, Eleanor."

The manor house as Dorset was ready—or as ready as Eleanor and her tiny household staff could make it in such a brief time. The servants had scrubbed the flagstones and beaten the worn rugs in the hall and bedchambers. Cobwebs were dusted away and the meagre plate polished. Parcels of dried herbs were hung about to sweeten the air and the privy flushed out with as much water as could be dragged from the well—a back-breaking and unpleasant job. Cook and some assistants plucked from the village had gone far afield to order fish and vegetables and spices…and that special requisite, the best wine. Eleanor was sorely glad Lord Warwick would be paying for it all.

She still did not know why such secrecy…or who was coming to her home. She assumed it would be her uncle himself, perhaps with his wife, her aunt Anne, and maybe Warwick's two small daughters, Isabel and Anne. Yet, it seemed to make no sense. None at all. The Earl never shown interest in her before.

"My Lady…" One of the young stable lads came running through the open door into the hall and dropped a swift bow. "Steward Grene has sent me to tell you that riders have been spotted coming toward the village."

"Thank you, Peter." Eleanor tried to keep her composure—why did she feel so unnerved? Dismissing the boy, she sat on her lonely seat on the raised dais at the end of the hall, thinking with sinking heart how the hall was a poor imitation of the grand banqueting hall she had known at Blakemere so long ago. The place looked shabby and slightly damp, and the Arras tapestries with their faded scenes of hunting and wine-making were frayed at the bottom. She stared down at her own gown; the hem was stained with mud where she had earlier walked through the courtyard—well, there was no time to change now, and her solitary tiring-woman, Agnes, was so fumble-fingered in her excitement over the mysterious guests-to-come, re-dressing would take far too long.

"Whoever comes with Warwick, he or she must take me as he finds me!" she murmured, lifting her chin and straightening her headdress, which she feared had gone slightly askew when she had fared outside earlier in the day to check that the stores were full and that the manor's cats and servants with stout shovels had cleared out the rats-nest she had spotted in a loft.

Outside she heard the burr of masculine voices and felt a pang of sadness, for she was reminded of the happier times when it would be Thomas, home from a visit to his parents at Sudeley, greeting the staff as he entered the hall. She tensed slightly, sat up straighter in her seat.

A man walked in; to her surprise, it was not her uncle Richard Neville but a stranger. Older than she, he had a weathered, friendly face and a gaze that, as it slid over her, was a little too familiar. Too appraising. She felt colour rise to her cheeks, but that moment Tom Montgomery arrived, moving quickly past the older man to bow before Eleanor's seat.

"My Lady, the party as described by Lord Warwick has arrived."

"And where is my uncle Warwick?" asked Eleanor. "Am I mistaken in some way? I assumed I would provide accommodation at Great Dorset for him and his guests."

"Forgive me if I gave that impression on our last meeting. It is not Lord Warwick who is here; he asked for your hospitality on his behalf but not for him."

Eleanor shifted uncomfortably. "Why do I feel as if I am being toyed with? I beg you, no more games. Who has my uncle sent to dwell beneath my roof?"

Tom Montgomery hesitated; the older man, still lingering in the back of the room, smiled, first at Eleanor and then at someone outside in the flambeaux-lit corridor.

"The lady is distressed…I must make my apologies." A third man entered the hall of Great Dorset manor, first clapping the older man upon the shoulder and then Tom. A flood of others followed in his wake—young squires, several pages, a series of proud-looking young fellows who appeared to be casually dressed but had swords bound at their side.

Eleanor peered at the man while attempting nonchalance—she did not wish to appear rude or forward. He was huge, possibly the tallest man she had ever beheld. And young, she guessed less than twenty summers old. Brown hair that held hints of gold and copper hung around a face that would not have seemed out of place in the romances favoured by Court ladies—a Lancelot, a Gawain, a Tristan.

He had a fair complexion with a long straight nose that turned up gently at the end and sparkling eyes that were neither light nor dark—a mixture of green, brown and gold. He was clad in garments of good value but not ostentatious; he was kitted out for the road.

Sudden nervousness gripped her, making her squirm. She knew her uncle's political affiliations but surely, he would not send *him* here...*Him*, of all people...

"Sir," her voice came out a shaky whisper, "I bid you give me your name since my uncle of Warwick has not."

The young man strode towards her seat, legs long and lithe, his shoulders massive beneath his Lincoln Green cloak. He still smiled, exuding charm, as he unexpectedly took a knee before her, clasped her hand and set his lips to it.

She was so startled by his forwardness, she nearly jerked her fingers away. She heard the older man who'd first entered with his entourage start to laugh then muffle the sound with a forced cough.

"My Lady Boteler," said the young man, "forgive me if I have discomfited you. Dick Neville should have spoken plainly to you. I am Edward...Edward of March."

Eleanor sat frozen, a statue of ice. It *was* him! Edward Plantagenet, the Duke of York's eldest son.

The enemy. Whose father's cause had wreaked Thomas's death; whose army had fought against her half-brother John, killing him along with Buckingham, Egremont and many other nobles. Edward...who, if the Act of Accord remained intact, might one day wear the crown, since it had been agreed that Duke Richard Plantagenet or his son should succeed Henry as heir to the throne!

"My Lord of March," she whispered. "This is a surprise indeed. I...I thought you were heading for Norfolk."

"Oh, so you have knowledge of my doings, Madam?" the young man roared with genial levity—and his followers laughed as he winked at them, their mirth ringing amidst the rafters.

Eleanor's cheeks burned furiously.

Edward swung back toward her, comely, merry. "It was originally my intention to visit the east, Lady, but of necessity, my plans had to change. I now head toward London to confer with my sire before he rides northward to his castle of Sandal. Unrest grows in the north; not all will accept him…" He shut his mouth with a snap, his expression growing suddenly hard. Then he glanced at Eleanor and smiled again. "I wish also to see my Lady Mother at Baynard's Castle, and I have two small brothers who I'm told are eager to see me. I have an older brother too, Edmund…but I rather doubt he'll be as eager to see me as they! At least, I expect he won't wish me to carry him about on my shoulders!"

The men behind him roared with mirth, the noise making Eleanor wince. She had lived a quiet life with Thomas, with none of this raucous behaviour even at Christmas.

"You do not smile," said Edward. "I seem to be offending you in some manner."

My husband died because of your father's desire to rule, she wanted to cry, but she was an intelligent woman— she knew it would be wise to hold back what was in her heart.

"You do not offend me, my Lord," she said carefully, "but you must understand—this is a small manor and a small village, and neither my household is not used to entertaining such esteemed company. How long do you plan to stay?"

"The lady wants rid of you already, Ned!" crowed the older man who seemed to be a close friend of March. He shook his head in mock sorrow. "You're losing your touch, Ned!"

"Hush, Will." Edward's mood changed slightly and his dark brows drew together; he cast his companion a warning look. "Forgive my friend, Will Hastings, Lady Eleanor. The winter wind chilled him while on the road and he availed himself of a skinful or two of wine. Now his tongue is wagging a bit too freely."

Eleanor arose from her place; next to Edward, she felt dwarfed, a small, dark, inconsequential creature, a mouse beside a great fierce lion ready to pounce. "There is food, as much as you need, and wine too, of course." She shot a hard look at the chastened Hastings. "All paid for by my uncle the Earl. My poor servants will tend to you and bring you meat and drink as you require. But I...I am not used to such high company and my husband has been dead but one bitter year. I would retire and bid you good night."

"You will not eat with us?" asked Edward. "Even if I were to ask you to stay?" He stepped a little closer to her; she could smell the scent he wore, frankincense mixed with clean sweat and horses, and for some reason, a strange, unnameable sensation gripped her body, making her breathing tight and her head giddy. Was she sickening with some unknown ailment?

Unsteadily, she clutched the arm of her chair; it was old, carved with roses. The Rose—it was a symbol of the House of York. Edward himself was named The Rose of Rouen for his great physical beauty. *The Rose...*

"No, I will not stay. Even if you ask me."

"What if I command it?"

"You may be of royal blood," she said, "but you are not a king to command."

An odd expression crossed Edward's face—slight annoyance mingled with mirth. "Lady...Well...you have heard of the Act of Accord surely. One day, God willing, who knows what I may be?"

She forced a brittle smile. "And then you can command me as you will, my Lord of March. Until then, I do as I will on my own lands."

Edward stepped aside as she made to pass him and descend from the dais. "I did not expect you would be so full of fire. I...I hope we will not be unfriends, Lady."

"Friends?" Her brows lifted. "I am a widow and many years your senior. It would not be proper. Good night, my Lord, may you feast merrily in my hall and eat well. If you need me at all, tell my steward Gilbert Grene to summon me. But I am sure you and your lords can sup and roister without an old dowager in your midst to mock."

Lifting her skirts, she stepped proudly through the hall. It had fallen so silent, she could hear her shoes clicking on the well-scrubbed tiles. She was relieved as she stepped from the chamber into the narrow corridor leading to the solar, lit by one solitary torch and with enough deep shadows to hide her flaming face.

Behind her, she heard a burst of laughter and then, moments later, the sounds of lutes, tabors and horns. Edward had brought his own travelling musicians with him for entertainment on the road. So arrogant!

She wondered if he had brought a Fool with him too. Perhaps she *was* the Fool, for she certainly had been fooled by her uncle of Warwick.

Hastily she made her way into her bedchamber, where she locked herself inside and knelt on her *pre dieu* under an old, battered bronze crucifix, praying to sweet Jesu that Edward of March would soon leave her home.

Even the weather conspired against Eleanor or so it seemed when she awoke the next morn. During the night, clouds had gathered and snow began to fall, thin flakes growing blizzard-like as the wind picked up. The area around Great Dorset was hilly and by dawn the heights were topped by white drifts. The track leading from the manor towards the village was white. Thin trails of smoke from the clustered peasants' cottages spiralled into the whitened air.

Entering the hall with some trepidation, she saw Edward sitting on her dais, *her* dais, eating sops from a bowl while his squires milled about him. As soon as he caught sight of her, his face brightened. "My Lady Eleanor," he said, "have you seen the weather outside?"

"Yes, of course."

Mournfully he shook his head. "Alas, my parents and my brothers must wait for me in Baynard's Castle. The weather is much too fierce to travel in."

Annoyance gripped Eleanor along with an unnerving sensation she could not name, one that twisted her belly into nervous knots. "Is it, my lord?" Her brows lifted. "To us, this dusting of snow is nothing! We see it every year on the hills. Everyone carries on as normal."

"Oh?" Edward took a handful of dried fruits from a page and thrust them into his mouth. Eleanor blinked. Did this huge man never stop eating? "I spoke to your Cook this morn. She said she'd never seen such deep snow so early. She was terrified she'd fall and break a leg just waddling across the courtyard!"

"You were talking to my *Cook*?" Eleanor blurted in surprise. What a strange creature this young man was, of royal lineage but wandering around talking to servants.

"And why not? She makes the delicacies that will go into my belly and the bellies of my friends. You must understand me, my Lady…" He suddenly became serious, sitting forward in his seat with an intent gaze—a gaze that pierced through her, transfixed her to the spot. It was as if all the air was thrust from her lungs, and she felt her ears ringing. "One day, if it be God's will, I might reign as King of England. Such are the terms of the Act of Accord. I do not believe Margaret of Anjou will accept those terms, but no matter…I will fight for them. And if ever I am crowned king, I swear I will be a different kind of king to those who have gone before. Open to my people and their complaints, *all* my people, not just the lords of the land. What do you think of that, Lady Eleanor?"

"I think…I think that would be…good," she gulped. "A ruler who is not a distant idol, kept away from his subjects. A king who will listen and will not be ruled by evil counsellors."

"So, by your statement, you admit King Henry is under the thumb of his wife and his advisers."

She shuddered, flushed; aware that all eyes were upon her. "I beg you, do not put words in my mouth.". I was ever loyal to King Henry, as was my father and my half-brother and my husband—who all died for his cause."

Edward's expression softened. "I believe you are a good woman, Eleanor."

Her blush deepened. "Not as good as I might be. I must away."

"Must you?" He was back to teasing, leaning back in Eleanor's seat, his legs splayed apart.

"Yes. I...I have my duties." Eleanor fled from the hall, feeling an outcast in her own home.

In her chamber, Eleanor sat fretfully embroidering. To her eyes, her work looked messy, haphazard—her mother would have beaten her if she'd made such poor stitches when learning needlework as a child. Her head throbbed with tension; behind her, Agnes brushed out the long dark waves of her hair. In shadow, the coils looked black as jet, yet the light from the window brought out flecks of burnished copper.

"What lovely hair you have, milady!" said Agnes, as she'd said a hundred times before when brushing her mistress' locks. Agnes was older and rotund and not graced with any beauty; she had a noticeable clubfoot and had hence never married. However, she was a loyal companion, whatever physical defects she had.

"My hair is as God made it, and I have no need for false flattery," snapped Eleanor waspishly, her mind ill at ease and desirous of quiet.

Agnes put down the brush, looking hurt. "Lady Eleanor, I meant every word; no falseness about it, I swear."

"Oh, Agnes." Eleanor let her embroidery fall to the floor and pressed her hands to her face. "Forgive me my harsh tongue. I...I am not myself with my house awash with...with strangers."

"I can understand your turmoil, Lady. All these men are unsettling—that one called Hastings tried to pinch my bottom!"

Did he, Agnes?" Eleanor forced back a small laugh. Yes, she could tell what type of man Will Hastings was…but *Agnes*? She doubted any man had ever paid court to Agnes in any way.

"He did indeed!" retorted the maid, "and I told him I was no harlot and he'd have to go to the nearest town for that sort of thing. And if he were to do it again, I'd take Cook's meat-cleaver to his…"

"Agnes, you did not!"

"I did, Lady, but he just laughed and strode away, proud as a peacock." Agnes pursed her lips. "However, if it had been the Lord Edward, maybe I would have welcomed his advances. Don't you think he's handsome, my Lady?"

Eleanor shifted uncomfortably on her cushioned stool. "Yes…no…Well, I do not really think on such things."

"You are such a pious and godly mistress." Agnes began plaiting her mistress's hair. "I can only hope to be as righteous and pure in mind and deed as you."

Eleanor's eyes narrowed. Was the maid mocking her? No, no…Agnes was a simple soul, who always spoke truth as she saw it.

"I shall be glad," said Eleanor, with a sigh, "when the Earl of March and his company are gone and my home is mine once more. Now, bring me my headdress and my good gown—the deep, rich red one with the squirrel fur trim. And the necklace with the trefoils set with garnets—bring it to me."

Agnes's dumpling-round visage lit up. "You *are* dressing up for someone, my Lady. Ah, you and the Lord Edward would make a handsome couple!"

"Agnes, enough!" Eleanor rolled her eyes. "Even were I interested in him, which I am not, he would never have me. I am older than he and have been married before. No doubt, his advisers will seek a fine match, perhaps a foreign princess."

"You are a highborn Lady," said Agnes loyally. "Your father was one of England's greatest champions and your mother is a Beauchamp, a family of great wealth and renown. Don't sell yourself short, Eleanor. After all, your sister Elizabeth married a Duke's son and she's younger than you. Why should you not marry as high, if not higher?"

"*Agnes*!" Eleanor warned again, ill at ease with the subject of the conversation. "I have not decided my future. Maybe I will never marry again. And if I do, it would certainly not be to the son of Richard Plantagenet." She gestured with some impatience to the wooden chest at the foot of her bed, which contained her best garments. "Come on, Agnes, no more idle chatter! Help me dress…"

"So where are you going, if you don't mind me askin'?"

"You're impertinent, Agnes, but I shall tell you. I am going to church!"

Eleanor hurried up the hill. Atop the height, loomed the deep red stones of All Saints Church. In the distance, sun smote the white-capped Burton hills and glanced off the rough ashlar blocks of a little watch tower set on the heights centuries ago, its fragmented machicolations glistening under white bands of snow. It was no longer inhabited and patches of decay dappled the conical roof; not far from its walls, to the north-west, stood the more modern Stonemilne, a windmill with sails that flapped in the wind. One of Thomas Boteler's ancestors had raised that windmill nigh on a hundred years ago.

Thomas… A cold feeling clutched her heart. For some reason, she could barely even envision his face anymore, yet little more than a year had passed since his death.

Feeling confused, she trudged on, her boots crunching on the snow, the only sound save for the soughing of the wind and the cries of distant birds.

No one from the village was up by the church and Eleanor hoped the priest would still be before the fire in his little stone cottage—she wanted to be alone with her thoughts.

Approaching the door, she grasped the iron-ring and turned it. The door creaked open, gliding inwards into the body of the church. Inside, all was still, but a few candles burned in cressets, casting a warm wavering light over the interior. A row of pillars marched down the nave towards the chancel arch and strange beings loomed out of the darkness—carvings of a winged monster with a human head lashing on its tail, and of a fearsome dragon battling a lion. These rubbed shoulders with more friendly beasts—a dog bounding after a hare, a squirrel clutching a nut, a proud, antlered stag and, appropriate since wool was the life's blood of Great Dorset, a sheep. There were other faces too, that smiled or grimaced in the gloom: two women in the headdresses and barbettes of olden times, a priest, a rat, and a wildman of the woods who held two pieces of greenery in his clenched hands.

Eleanor took a step forward. Her boots leaked trails of melted snow on the tiles underfoot, brightly coloured, decorated with lions. Outside the sun moved from behind a cloud, shining through the clear glass windows in their neat arched frames. Eleanor had always wondered why Lord Sudeley had removed the coloured glass but today, perhaps, she learnt why. The sunlight flooded in, illuminating the paintings over the Chancel arch—the Virgin Mary, beautiful and serene, with St John at her side and censer-bearing angels standing sentinel behind them.

Eleanor hastened to a little chapel in the north aisle. It was close, private, a holy place. A depiction of one of the Three Magi gazed solemnly down at her from the wall. Arranged around the doorframe, a painted tracery of red flowers gave the chantry a slightly more secular touch. Eleanor knelt before the altar. Her breath came out in white puffs before her lips; the church was cold, its snowed roof shaded by encircling trees on the northern side. *Dear Jesu and Blessed Mary, in your mercy smile on me and help me, a wicked woman, to show generousness to the men I house, no matter how I resent them. I know it is good to show charity and to pray for their souls, even if I care not for their business. Grant me strength to always be the best I can be, residing in your Light, chaste and pure with no temptations....*

She halted in her prayer. Temptations? What was she thinking of? She had no temptations at Great Dorset, nor would she ever, God willing. One day she might marry again but not now, she could not bear to even think of such an event, with Thomas not long in his grave in St Alban's, a grave she had not even visited...

LIAR...A hard, mocking little voice sounded in her brain. *You pretend but God can see your heart. You are not pure. You are nought but a 'Holy Harlot'.*

Clumsily she rose, blushing in shame, sure that at this very moment God was frowning upon her from his eternal Throne. Overhead, Christ on the Rood, his brow pierced by thorns, gazed in agony towards his Father in Heaven as if He suffered for Eleanor's innate sinfulness... She was appalled. Had she lost her wits in her widowhood?

She made to turn, to fly from the little chantry chapel into the nave with its almost pagan carvings, but then she heard the door-ring turn. A splash of winter light fell across the tiles, making the lions on the tiles roar to life and the angels on the chancel arch turn a deep rose hue.

She swallowed as a figure blocked the light, shadow stretching long into the gloomy interior of the church. Was it Father Gray? She could scarcely bear to face him, the confess her wicked thoughts.

Another fear gripped her, making her heart begin to beat fast and hard. She had strolled away from the manor without even a solitary attendant as she was wont to do in such a small village, its population so depleted since the last century's Black Death that she knew every last soul living there. Yet there were now strange men at the manor, there at her invitation, fighting men who may not have been with a woman for months—hard-bitten men who might even think it resourceful to abduct a widow of good blood with a few lands to her name.

She halted in her tracks, peering around for something she might use as a weapon if necessary. God's House offered nothing. She would just have to hope the newcomer was benign and not of evil thought and deed.

"Who...who is there?" she called out, attempting to keep her voice steady. Since Thomas's demise, she had learnt in her dealing with the villagers that it was perilous to show any fear; one must maintain an air of calm control at all times in difficult situations.

"Lady Eleanor, have I startled you?" A voice sounded in her ears and now her heart truly began to pound, galloping like a horse in full flight.

The door drifted shut, the exterior light was cut off, passing snow clouds veiled the sun and turned the windows dim—she stood in the gloom with Edward of March. Tall Edward with his broad shoulders and his smooth, unlined face, the visage of an angel... *Or was it a tempting devil?*

"No, no, you did not startle me!" she barked, realising how unconvincing she sounded even as the words grated from her throat.

He smiled a long lazy smile. Shadowed, his eyes, looked dark in the church's gloom, but they glittered a little beneath his straight brows. Hard diamonds.

"Is there something you wish?" Eleanor plucked up courage.

"Can a man not pray in a church?" he said, his smile widening.

"I presumed you would use my chapel. You and your men have used everything else..." She shut her mouth with a snap. No matter what she thought of his father's claim to the throne and the Act of Accord forced on Henry and Margaret, Edward was still a prince of the blood. And she had been rude, not just rude but recklessly, foolishly so. Harsh words spoken imprudently often ignited feuds far worse than the words themselves.

He cast back his head and laughed. It seemed the most awful and yet strangely wonderful sound in the world. "You are no wilting flower, are you, Eleanor? Despite your show of piety?"

"Show? I *am* pious," she said with a trace of anger. "I try to follow the word of Christ as best I may. Sometimes I fail for I am a sinner…"

"I, too, am a sinner," said Edward. His tone was silk.

I'll warrant you are indeed, she thought, staring up at him.

"It is not right we have this discourse in a sacred place," she said firmly. "My lord, let us go outside."

"As you wish…and you may cease to call me 'my lord.' You need not be so formal. Call me Edward. Or Ned."

"I will do no such thing, *my lord*. It's not proper!"

She swirled past him, eager for the door and freedom beyond. Bursting out into the harsh wintry light, she breathed in the snow-tinged air. Edward was beside her in an instant, his shadow enveloping her, embracing her. She began to shiver, despite the warmth of her cloak with its squirrel trim.

"Do not be afraid," said Edward. "I am a knight. I wish you no harm. It is my sworn duty to *protect* widows."

She said nothing but drew her cloak more tightly about her shoulders. Edward strode ahead a few paces, gazing out across the landscape. "It is beautiful here."

"Yes," she said.

"I would fain dwell in peace in such a place."

"Oh, I doubt you would, my lord…Edward. I have no doubt you'd be bored beyond belief without jousting and banquets and the intrigues of the court. You would not chase your enemies in battle—you'd end up chasing sheep instead!"

He put his hands on his hips, playful. "And would I not make a goodly shepherd?

"I deem you'd be a better warrior. I think the sheep would be afraid of you."

He let out a bellow of laughter, then fell silent again, arms now folded. The pallid daylight struck on the rings on his fingers; they glimmered with red, blue and green lights. He looked at the ground. "Evil weather or no, I have decided to leave your manor on the morrow, Lady Eleanor."

"Oh." Her breath rushed out.

"My father, it seems, is getting ready to ride north; he may need to leave to leave London in haste. I cannot tarry."

"I understand, my lord."

"Do you? I don't think you do. Sweet, naive Eleanor, widow of the wilds!"

"I beg you, Edward—don't mock me."

"I do not. I will say only this…the hill upon which we stand is beautiful, that and the land around it. And you too are beautiful to my eyes, and it will pain me to leave so soon."

"Maybe it is for the best, my lord," she said. "For both of us."

"Ah, there she is, the pious little lady of Great Dorset again, but I can see in her eyes that she is not a flower stricken by frost, ever cold and unwelcoming. God, Eleanor, you must know I want you…"

He reached for her, his hands coming down hard on her upper arms; she could feel the bite of those ringed fingers. She froze like a wild deer faced by a hunter.

"No, my lord, Edward, no! You say you are a good knight and true, a protector of women. If you truly are what you say, let me go."

Immediately Edward's hands fell to his sides. The sun slid behind one of the hills, burning red; blue, delicate light descended, wrapping trees, church tower and the tall prince of the House of York in a dimming haze.

"I will go, for now," said Edward, "but I would not be surprised if we should meet again in the future, God willing. That's what you are waiting for, is it not, my little Eleanor? The blessing of God upon whatever you do?"

He gave her no chance to answer but began to stride in the direction of the manor house. He never looked back.

She stood alone on the hilltop in the cold and the growing dark, her cloak billowing in a rising wind. She stayed there till old Father Gray stumbled up the hill, puffing, a lantern swinging from his gnarled hand, ready for Vespers. The villagers followed in his wake, a stream of dark figures, rushlights clutched in their hands against the encroaching darkness.

Eleanor followed Father Gray back inside the church. Suddenly she felt sorely in need of absolution.

CHAPTER SIX

January hung over Warwickshire like a grey and water-logged rag. The earlier snows had departed but skies were leaden and trees skeletons raised knobbly arms toward an unfriendly sky. Eleanor was crossing the manor's courtyard toward the kennel, to take out her Talbot hound, Blanchette, when she noticed a disturbance amidst the houses in the street beyond the open gate. People were milling about in the centre of the road, jostling each other in excitement.

News. It had to be some kind of news of great import. Attaching Blanchette's lead to her collar, Eleanor began to walk briskly towards the gateway. Even as she approached the open wooden doors, a figure on horseback broke away from the crowd in the street and rode towards her at a brisk trot.

She halted. The newcomer was a man in dark leather, caked from head to toe in mud from the road. His horse had been grey; it was brown now, save for where lather had stripped the mud away. "Halt!" she cried as the man drew abreast of her. Close, he was wild-eyed, almost mad-looking, the whites of his eyes bright against the muddied planes of his face. "Who are you? What is your business here?"

"I am a messenger bringing news from the north. I carry word of momentous deeds to all the places where I ride. I must see the master of this place."

"There is no master. However, I am mistress of the manor of Great Dorset. You may speak to me. What is your news?"

"A battle has been fought in the north, my Lady. A great battle at Wakefield."

Eleanor's mouth went dry. Had Edward of March gone north? No, he said he was heading to London, to see his father and brother before they fared out to quash rebellion. "What was the outcome of this battle, messenger?"

"Richard, Duke of York is slain and his son Edmund Earl of Rutland with him. Salisbury was also taken and executed at Pontefract. Queen Margaret has ordered their heads set upon the gates of York."

Eleanor went cold. She thought of Edward of March sitting in her hall, laughing as he spoke of his brother Edmund. She reckoned the lad must have been no more than seventeen years old. "What...what of Edward?" the words slipped from between her chilled lips.

The messenger misunderstood her, thinking she spoke of Edward of Lancaster, Henry VI's young son. "The prince will now be restored to his rightful position as heir to the kingdom. I have heard her Grace the Queen is ecstatic. God be praised that York has fallen."

Eleanor flushed. "Yes...y...yes," she stammered, "Prince Edward."

"God save his grace King Henry!" said the courier with stalwart enthusiasm

"God save King Henry," she repeated, her voice dull. All she could think of was more blood spilt, a seventeen-year-old boy.... And on the other side of the conflict, *her* side, her half-brother John, her husband Thomas, both hacked to death on the field. So much blood...and Edward, Edward of March, not the six-year-old Prince of Wales—he would want vengeance for his slain kin. Terrible bloody vengeance.

The messenger was looking at her expectantly. "Are you hale, madam?" he asked. "You look...unwell."

"I am just overwhelmed by the news, coming so soon after Christmas."

"Aye." The man grinned. "The Yorkists will have had a miserable Yule. With any luck, what's left of them will do the right thing and scurry off to exile."

"Let us just pray for peace—peace for all," murmured Eleanor. *It will not happen, not in my lifetime, I think...*

"Amen to that," said the messenger without much conviction. "Now I must be on my way to carry the message of the defeat of the King's enemies throughout the land."

He did not move. At Eleanor's side, Blanchette gave a ferocious little growl. Then she realised what the messenger was waiting for: payment for bringing his tidings of the battle.

Reaching to the small purse affixed to her girdle, Eleanor pulled out a few coins. She had scarcely brought them out when the man's gloved hand was stretching in her direction.

"For your tidings, sir," she said, dropping the coins into his palm with a clink. He stared down his nose at them, clearly disappointed there were not more, then gave a grunt and dug his heels into his horse's flanks. The beast lurched forward and he wheeled it around, yanking cruelly on the bit. Blanchette gave a loud bark and lunged forward; Eleanor hauled the hound back by her collar.

Then she was running up towards the gate of the manor house, sliding in the mud, Blanchette bounding beside her, white ears flapping in the wind of her speed. *Edward will want revenge!* Her mind screamed over and over. The Queen's army had slain the Duke of York, but in doing so they would rouse his son, young and full of fire and impetuosity.

In striking down Richard of York, the House of Lancaster had reaped the whirlwind.

Edward, now Duke of York after the death of his sire, stood in the market square of Hereford with Will Hastings, Sir Walter Devereux, Lord Grey of Wilton, Sir William Herbert and his old friend Richard Croft, who had known him from his youth at the castle of Ludlow.

Dusk was falling, casting a gloomy blue light over the streets; crowds of townsfolk, ethereal as wraiths, drifted by in haloes of torchlight. Armoured men strode alongside them, keeping them quiet and subdued—and away from Edward and his commanders.

In the centre of the square stood a scaffold, empty now, the executioners having finished their gory task. Blood stained the platform and steps and ran in rivulets around the cobblestones, mingling with the thin snowflakes that had started to fall from on high.

It was early February, Candlemas, Feast of the Presentation of the Infant Jesus, and all over the town candles burned in windows and in churches and at the cathedral of St Mary the Virgin and St Ethelbert the King.

They also glowed, melting into pools of tallow, all over the market cross, up the worn steps, to ring the base of the cross itself. And there, limned by the fluttering light, a madwoman with straggling hair and tearful eyes keened as she held a severed head in her arms. Lovingly she combed the blood-matted hair and beard, kissed the sightless eyes and gaping grey mouth.

It was the head of Owen Tudor, captured after the battle and summarily executed.

Edward glanced dispassionately towards the macabre sight. "He lay his head once in the lap of a Queen, so he told us before he died. Now he has a madwoman for company instead."

Hastings laughed. "I could use a woman for company. But not a crazed one like that crone!"

Something flashed in Edward's eyes, quickly dulled. "There will be time for such merriment later, Will. But not now. We must find out the moves of Margaret and our enemies, and if we can, make haste to London to keep her from the city. Whoever holds London shall surely hold England."

"And you will be proclaimed King there," said Will, suddenly serious.

"Yes, I shall be King," said Edward, his gaze steely. "Did you not see the Parhelion on the battlefield, Will? The Three Suns in the Sky—the Trinity. The three sons of York my father, who lies dead in Blackfriars in Pontefract. Dead and headless...like *him*." He nodded toward the grotesque spectacle upon the cross in Hereford Market Square. "God on high has shown us his will—even if the Lancastrians have not yet realised it. The House of York shall rule." His hard, young face softened a little. "It is a long journey to London, though, Will, and the winter fights foul against us. I am sure I can find us a comfortable place to stop upon the way…Christ, there may even be a pair of comfortable arms, if I'm lucky!"

"What about me?" said Will, pretending to be cross with his long-time friend.

"You can have the blowzy old washerwoman," laughed Edward, setting his spurs to the flanks of his mount. "If she'll have you!"

Spring had come to Great Dorset. Trees raised their arms toward a strengthening sun, the first hints of buds gleaming like tiny emeralds on their boughs. The hills went from white to brown to faintly green, and sheep clustered by old Lord Sudeley's windmill and the turreted watchtower, where they sheltered in their lee.

Eleanor felt as if she walked in a strange dream as she walked up the hill towards the church. The shocking news of the Duke of York's death early in January had been replaced by the news of his son's victory at Mortimer's Cross. It was not a decisive victory, though—a few weeks later uncle Warwick had fought the Queen's army at St Alban's and been routed, although he escaped with his life. King Henry, Warwick's prisoner, had been released and his guards, Lord Bonville and the aged veteran Sir Thomas Kyriell, were executed before Margaret and young Prince Edward, who had been goaded by his mother into clamouring for their deaths. The King, doddering in his dirty robes, his hair and beard matted and straggling like those of a mad prophet, had then knighted his little son, who in turn knighted thirty men for loyal service.

Eleanor hesitated a moment, closing her eyes. The wan sun, barely warm, beat on her eyelids. Thirty more knights for Lancaster…which she had once sworn to support. Thirty more men to go to future battle because she knew the war was not over. Margaret would never rest while Edward remained alive, and Edward's revenge for the slaying of his father and brother would not be complete until Henry was cast down and Margaret subdued. As for the young Prince of Wales…

"There is peace here at Great Dorset," she murmured. "He will never come here again. Why should he? He is a man schooled to war, used to mighty strongholds and great palaces, to the councils of lords…and, so I hear, the delights of beautiful women. Why would he come back here? There is no reason. None. I hope he never returns to disrupt Dorset's peace, *my* peace…"

She opened her eyes again as the skeleton of a dry old leaf, left over from winter, blew across her cheek, its touch soft as a caress. She lied to herself. She wanted her peace, but she wished to see the young Duke of York too. Why, she did not quite understand; he was her opposite in all ways. The Sunne in Splendour, the handsome Rose of Rouen, most beautiful prince. By contrast, she was the Night, dark and silent, dedicated to the lily and rose of the Virgin…

What she wished for in her deepest, darkest dreams was not right, but all the prayers for constancy and chasteness that she made before Our Lady's image availed her nought. Her heart knew the truth, as wicked as it was. Mind warred against traitorous body—and her body, and heart, won.

Walking onwards, she approached the Holy Well that bubbled out of a green bank near the church. A small, lichen-bound stone canopy arched over it; offerings of dried flowers and burnt out candles lay around it, as they had done time out of mind. An old woman was kneeling by its side, peering into the water; Eleanor recognised Godelive, one of the oldest villagers in Dorset. She had delivered most of the babies in the area and when younger was a noted herbalist. Now, she had gone blind in one eye and her mind had failed, and she wandered through the village singing and mumbling words to unseen shades of those long dead. She was singing now, her toothless mouth working, her arthritic hands knotting and unknotting.

"In the Apocalypse Saint John
Gazed on a woman crowned with the Sunne,
The moon under her feet shone,
Twelve stars on her brow were bound...."

A shiver ran down Eleanor's spine; she could not quite fathom why. "Godelive, if you wish to speak of the Book of Revelations, you should seek the priest. If you are fearful of that Last Day, Father Gray will comfort you."

Godelive raised her shaggy grey head and gazed blearily at Eleanor. "Don't need no priest, had too much o' priests, Lady. Come closer, dear, come closer, and look into the well. It is flowing after the hard ice of winter, flowing like the Virgin's tears, her Holy milk. In its pure heart, it shows many great things destined by God!"

Eleanor was half-minded to run away from the gibbering crone but her position as Lady of the Manor made it impossible. Old Godelive was her tenant, her responsibility. She must be strong. Coming up to the rim of the pond next to the ancient woman, she stared into the softly bubbling water.

Godelive groped at her hanging sleeve, excited. "Do you see it, Lady? Do you see it?"

"I see my own reflection," laughed Eleanor, "nothing more. You need to go home, Godelive. Your daughter Parnel will be worrying about you up here on the hillside."

"Lady, Lady, no, you must see!" cried Godelive, becoming agitated. "Look with your heart, not just with your eyes. "

The woman was so upset, her withered frame shaking like a leaf in the wind, that Eleanor decided to humour her. She glanced back into the well, at her solemn, dark-eyed reflection. Above her head, the spring sun burst from behind a cloud and haloed her head, shooting out rays into the blue sky like the tines upon a coronet.

She jumped back in fright. "You saw, didn't you! You saw!" Godelive capered about, flailing her bony arms. "Crowned with the Sunne. So it will be!"

Eleanor hastily pulled away from the dancing crone. Above her, the emergent sun was furled once more in a shroud of fast-moving cloud. Shadows dappled the Burton hills. And a sound came from the village below, the sound of people hollering and cheering, followed by the brazen notes of a trumpet. A trumpet that called over and over again.

Eleanor ran back onto the path and stared down the hill, amidst the thatched rooves with their thin chimneys trickling blue-dark smoke. Between them, banners were unfurling. She recognised, as her belly knotted in both fear and elation, the Falcon and Fetterlock and the White Rose of York. But they were not the only banners; above all was an unfamiliar one, bearing the image of a rayed sun, and next to it, in a bold statement, flew the Arms of England, unquartered.

Eleanor sat in the Great Hall of her manor house, in the position her status dictated but at her side sat the man who would be shortly proclaimed King of England. He had told her with his own lips he was on his way to London for a hasty proclamation of his position as King.

"There are two Kings at present," he was saying, not so much to Eleanor but to his eager circle of attendants, "and Christ knows why, but Mad Harry still has his followers. They will not give up yet, I fear."

"It is Margaret," said Will hasting, "that French she-wolf. She's fighting not for the moon-mad old man but the boy. Her precious son, Edward of Westminster."

Edward made a dismissive gesture. "The child probably isn't even Mad Harry's. The brat may be the get of Edmund Beaufort, Duke of Somerset."

"Aye!" cried Hastings. "No doubt that randy Frenchwoman put the cuckold's horns on that old loon on the throne." He put his hands up to his head, curving his fingers into a semblance of horns, and began to caper about on the dais, while he cried in an affected voice, "Oh, Margaret, how did our son get here again? It must have been through magic! Or through the agency of the Holy Ghost!"

The men in the chamber burst into laughter, many of them deep in their cups. Eleanor sat in silence, filled with shame. She'd always been loyal to the sovereigns, as her family loyalties dictated, and here were Edward's men openly mocking them.

She glanced at Edward, sitting in a short doublet of crimson velvet trimmed with fur and golden thread, dark violet hose stretched over his muscular thighs, his hat worn at a jaunty angle, his brown hair combed glistening to touch his shoulders. He was as far away from sad, limp old Harry Six as a man could be. Henry was the past, a troubled past filled with loss of French lands and England's decline; Edward was the future, a new dawn, the sun rising brightly over a waiting land.

Her gaze touched the new badge on his doublet; a rayed sunburst. He seemed to sense her attention; swivelling away from the loonish antics of Hastings, he smiled in her direction. "My Lady Eleanor, I fear I have not given you the regard you deserve this evening. It is a pleasure to make your acquaintance again, here in Great Dorset. Much has come to pass since last I imposed upon your hospitality."

"So I have heard," said Eleanor. "Your badge...it is new. I did not recognise your banner when first I saw it unfurled."

"The Sunne...the Sunne in Splendour." Edward's hand closing around the badge. "I saw Three Suns before the battle at Mortimer's Cross, a sign that God was with me. I decided to use that emblem as my own from that day forward."

"God may be with you, your Grace, but Margaret of Anjou will never give up as long as..."

"As she is free and her husband and son also? Yes, you are right. Even in the wake of Mortimer's Cross, she was defiant and managed to defeat Warwick at St Alban's. Thank Jesu, Dick escaped with his life."

Eleanor crossed herself. Her uncle had always been lucky in battle—so far.

"I was prepared to give battle again, weary as my army was, but then I learnt of wondrous happenings, Eleanor. Despite her victory at St Alban's, Margaret could not persuade London to open its gates to her forces. The Londoners despise her and fear the way she cannot keep her dogs of men under control. They have no such fear of me; they await my entrance to the city with joy. I shall be proclaimed King, Eleanor, and none shall withstand me; if England must run red with blood for my throne to be made secure, then so it must be."

Eleanor went cold, then hot. Edward was looking at her most intently, in a way to which she was unaccustomed. Even Thomas had never gazed upon her with such open *desire,* not even in the first heady days of their marriage. They had known each other so long, been betrothed for so many years, they sometimes were more like brother and sister than lovers as they went about the mundane events of their life together.

Edward of York was different. This intense young man was everything Thomas had never been. Handsome, impetuous, ruthless…*and soon to be King of England.*

"Eleanor," Edward suddenly said in a quiet voice, leaning towards her. "I came here on my way to London not just because it was the best route to take. I came to see you. I could not stop thinking about you since our last meeting."

She folded her hands and stared at them, unwilling to meet his eyes. "Your Grace flatters me. I am sure he had much more on his mind the past few months than a lowly widow in Warwickshire."

"Why do you call yourself 'lowly'? I do not see you as such. Your sister is wed into the Mowbrays, my friends and supporters. Your father was of high lineage and considered a hero while he lived."

"I do not know what you wish of me, your Grace." Eleanor glanced up but still would not meet Edward's gaze full on. She stared out into the hall, taking deep breaths.

"Do you not? I do not think you ignorant. Are you playing coy or are you in truth not made of normal woman's flesh but of a nunly bent?"

"I am not a harlot, if that's what you ask, my lord," said Eleanor sharply, "and I follow the laws of God as set out for mankind in the Holy Bible." She raised her hand to finger the tiny silvered cross with green paste jewels that hung about her neck; a comfort in those uncomfortable moments.

"So you do, to my regret." Edward gave a low, rueful chuckle, and he turned away and began to talk animatedly with William Hastings.

He did not speak to Eleanor for the rest of the evening. For some reason that vexed Eleanor much more than it should have, and she was distinctly relieved when Edward, unsteady on his feet after imbibing much wine with his friends, called a halt to the banquet and sought the quarters she had supplied. Watching him leave the hall, listening to his laughter and that of his companions as it faded into the distance, she was gripped again by inner conflict. Eager to set her thoughts elsewhere, she began to pace about the hall helping the servants begin the clean-up, scraping away gnawed bones and collecting the trenchers into a basket where, sodden with gravy, they would be delivered to the poorest folk in the village.

"Milady, you don't have to do any of this!" said Cook, in surprise, as Eleanor filled a basket, all the while dripping gravy down her gown.

"Yes, I do," murmured Eleanor. "I must remember my place and not seek to rise above it, nor must I shirk the duties, both on this earth and in Heaven, to which I am sworn."

The sun was still abed, lying low behind the ridge of hills. Eleanor rose from beneath her warm coverlet with its embroideries of Talbots—white hounds just like faithful Blanchette, who was curled in a woven basket in the corner. Eleanor kept her close now, rather than in the kennels—a non-judgmental friend, a warm comfort.

In the brazier the fire was nearly out; Agnes snored on her pallet before the glowing embers, a sheepskin over her slumbering form, although one stubby leg thrust out onto the chill ground. Breath hanging in the air, Eleanor managed to wrestle a gown over her kirtle. It was bitterly cold; it chilled the bone. The young woman felt glad, as if rising this early was providing a kind of mortification of the flesh. One she sorely needed.

Carefully, she lit a small candle and placed it in the lantern on the table. The lantern had been a gift from Lord Sudeley; wrought from beaten bronze, its frontage was constructed of clear horn to allow the light to shine forth. Carefully she lifted it; the fluttering light danced about the room, making both Blanchette and Agnes stir in their sleep.

But neither awoke.

Down, down the stairs, Eleanor stole in that early hour. She had drawn on her soft boots for she expected she might encounter mud; rain had fallen in the night, she had heard the lulling drum on the manor house roof, up above the ancient beams with their web-festooned carvings from long ago.

She was heading to the church, as she so often did when unease of mind gripped her. As she had done before when Edward was in her house. The same situation, yet so different from before. *He was a man who would be a king, his throne won in blood...*

The church loomed ahead, dark against the lighter backdrop of the sky. Drizzle fell, cold and cheerless. The tree branches clacked, their boughs still barely sprouted after the winter; her fluttering candle, safe within the embrasure of the lantern, was the only light in all the world.

Somewhere she heard a fox yelp; it made the hairs on the back of her neck stand up and for a moment she wished she'd brought Blanchette, but she knew no one in the village would mean her harm.

And then she heard it, footsteps on the grass. Just as she had heard them before, but here it was near daybreak, near the coming of the sun, instead of at dusk.

Without looking, she knew. It was him. She stood still as a stone, her mantle flapping in the chill north-eastern wind, waiting.

He came up behind her, voice soft silk in her ear, his breath warm, slightly spiced with wine from the evening before. "Eleanor."

"You followed me again, your Grace. As before. I am here only to seek God; I would prefer no other distraction. I beg you, return to the manor."

"Am I such a distraction then?" There it was again in his voice, that warm, mocking merriment. "Maybe I want to pray too, for the way ahead is still unclear and the times uncertain. I do have a modicum of piety, you know…"

"My chapel in the manor and my chaplain are at your disposal. I informed you of that."

"I saw your light. I did not like the idea of you going off in the dark alone, unaccompanied by even a maid."

"Oh, I am quite safe here. I have never felt fearful in Great Dorset."

"Are you fearful of me?"

She hesitated. "No. I…I believe you to be honourable." Her heart began to thud; her cheeks felt hot despite the cold morning.

Edward's hand came up, drawing back her hood. She had left her hair uncovered, due to her haste and the earliness of the hour. "Your hair is like the raven's wing; I guessed it would be."

His fingers tangled in the darkness of her locks, freeing them from the hood. The wind lifted the dark mass, hurling it across her face. "Your Grace, I beg you…it is immodest…"

"You are too beautiful to worry about such things as modesty!"

"But God…"

"He gave you your fairness, did he not? Surely you do not question Our Maker's judgement?"

Eleanor made to retort but Edward laid a finger over her lips. She gasped at the intimacy of his touch, his sword-calloused finger on her mouth. "No more arguments. Listen to what I have to say. In the days that follow I will be proclaimed King, but the Lancastrians will mass against me and I have no doubt I must soon fight again. I pray I will be given the ultimate victory but the Wheel of Fortune turns in ways unforeseen. I would not go from here without having had some solace…in you…"

"Edward…" As his hands descended on her shoulders, then slid to her arms, tightening, she shook her head. "You…your Grace, you demean me, I will not."

"I think I can persuade you. I have seen the flower of womanhood in your eyes. You were never meant to live as a nun…" His grip on her arms tightened. She tried to pull back but his hold was strong as steel.

"I beg you…" she implored, but as his head bowed to hers, she found herself yielding to the pressure of his hands and then his seeking lips. To her horror, she found her own arms stretching around Edward's back, not thrusting him away but drawing him even closer. As the sun began to rise over the rim of the world, drenching both man and woman with incarnadine light, they kissed with unbridled passion on the broad hillside near the ancient Holy Well, in the lee of the church of All Saints.

"Eleanor, I beg, you…be my mistress." The words came hastily, harshly, between breathless kisses.

The word mistress brought Eleanor to earth with a thud. She tore her mouth away from Edward's and brought her hands around to lie against his broad chest—still touching him, but ready to resist should he try to embrace her violently again.

"No," she croaked. Her voice sounded as harsh as that of the crows who, woken by the burgeoning light, squabbled in the nearby trees. "I will be no man's mistress."

"Not even a King of England?" Edward stepped away from her so abruptly she nearly fell forward. The dawn-light reddened his face; he looked angry, maybe even dangerous.

"No," she said. "Not even a King of England. I heed the words of the King of Kings, not Kings wrought of mortal flesh."

"Damn you, you are overbold in your talk, Madam."

She winced as she heard the barely restrained rage in his voice. But still she spoke, attempting to keep her composure, "Not so bold as you, I fear, your Grace. Now, let us speak no more of things that cannot, must not be."

Edward began to stalk around the hilltop, circling Eleanor with long, agitated strides—*like a beast circling prey*, she thought. "What can I give you, that you will be mine?" he asked. "Lands, gifts—name it and it will be yours!" He gestured to the church behind them, its stones now painted rosy by the dawn. "Your little church, of which you seem so proud—I noticed the tower needs repair. The roof is worn; soon rain will drip inside. Once I am secure on the throne that is mine by right, I will pay for repairs on Great Dorset church, Eleanor—if you will be my light o' love. Yes, yes, and on top of that, I will send a loaf of bread to each man, woman and child in the village!"

"I cannot deny the church is in poor repair; I have limited resources to pay for a mason for extensive work. But I will not sell myself for Great Dorset…for the church…for anyone."

Edward looked fit to explode. "Your coldness to me belies your kiss. Have you no liking for me at all?"

Eleanor gazed sorrowfully at her feet. "The problem is, I have too much liking for you, your Grace. But I have a greater liking for my honour and for what is right and good."

"What would make you change your mind?"

"Nothing. I will be no man's mistress. I will lie down with a man only if it is within wedlock according to God's Law."

Edward's breath railed through his teeth. "But I…I dare not…Christ, you vex me with this pious foolishness! I would take care of you, you know that."

"You would, I am sure, but *I* must take care of my immortal soul. I will not live in sin even with the King of England."

"You want marriage." Edward's tone was gruff. "Then marriage it will have to be, for I want you and will not be gainsaid. Tomorrow I leave for London. When all is said and done and my crown assured, I will return for you. Mark my words and ready yourself, I will return."

Whirling on his heel, he stormed off into the red morning, vanishing amidst the mist-clouds that began to rise as the sun warmed the frigid ground.

Eleanor placed her fingers to her lips, bruised from the urgent insistence of his mouth, and felt her eyes fill with tears. She would be Edward's wife—if he should survive the inevitable and final battle for the throne.

And as his wife that meant she, daughter of the esteemed Earl of Shrewsbury, would be, beyond all belief, made a Queen….

CHAPTER SEVEN

Under the snow, the dead men lay, mouths gaping in silent, eternal screams. Under the snow, the blood of the Red Rose seeped into the frozen ground and fed the hungry earth.

The Battle of Palm Sunday at Towton had been fought upon the 9th day of March, with unseasonal snow flurries blowing into the faces of the Lancastrians, giving the Yorkist army the advantage. The icy field had become a killing ground where men were hunted like beasts, then felled with many blows…and all the rivers ran red for days.

Edward of York was victorious, his kingship, first proclaimed in London in February, now a firm reality. The Lancastrian Lords Dacre, Westmoreland, Clifford, Neville, Maulay and Welles were slain. Sir Andrew Trollope, who betrayed Richard of York at Ludford Bridge, died in the slaughter too. Henry Percy, Earl of Northumberland, fled to York and there expired of grievous wounds. Old King Henry, his Queen and their seven-year-old son fled away toward the Scottish border, seeking refuge.

Within the castle of York, Edward sat surrounded by his nobles, including his favourites Warwick, Hastings, and William Neville Lord Fauconberg. Battered and bruised by the terrible battle, yet the men there were all merry. The sun had risen over England after a dark long winter.

"Although King Henry yet lives, his power is shattered," said Edward. "He will not have the power to rise against me again, nor will the she-wolf who flees at his side."

"And the boy?" queried Lord Fauconberg.

Edward shrugged a muscled shoulder, wincing slightly; he was bruised from delivering mighty blows upon his defeated enemies in the rout at Towton. "He is not even quite the age of my brother Richard. It will be years before I need worry about him, if I ever do. For now, we rest—then we leave for London to plan my Coronation."

"And when will you seek the assumption of the crown?" asked Lord Hastings

"Much must be done in advance of the day; rebels still trouble Kent and their risings must be put down. I hope that I may be crowned at Westminster near the end of June at the latest. In the days when the sun shines strongest, may a Sunne rise over all England." He smiled at his own joke.

Then he turned to Will, a mysterious expression on his face. "I have other business to attend to first, though. In Warwickshire."

"Eh, what is this I hear about Warwickshire?" Richard Neville, Earl of Warwick, swivelled around upon his bench.

"It is nought, Dick." Edward clapped his cousin of Warwick on the shoulder. "A private joke between Hastings and myself...*More wine*!" Without meeting Warwick's probing gaze, the young king bellowed to a page standing at attention nearby. "Quickly now, Bertrand. More wine for all my loyal lords!"

Warwick's face grew dark and troubled. "It's a woman, isn't it, Ned? Always a woman. *That* sort of business."

Grinning, Edward raised his goblet. "It is good to be King!"

"You must look to more than wenches to be a successful King." An angry little blue vein began to pulse on Warwick's temple.

Edward slung back the wine and wiped his lips. "And so I shall...but I will not live like any monk. After all, *you* have not, have you, Dick?"

The Earl sputtered in indignation. "If you refer to my baseborn daughter Margaret, she was born in my years of youthful folly, and I would not play false to my Duchess, Anne. Even so, I am not a King, and who I bed is not important in the scheme of things. Some women can lead a man into dire trouble." Warwick folded his arms over his chest, belligerent, eyes burning in sockets darkened by days of little sleep. "Remember your position, Edward, fought for with so much loss. Be careful where you sow your lusts."

"Well, this is frank talk indeed to your sovereign," laughed the young ruler, half-teasing his kinsman—but not entirely jesting. A certain hardness touched his clear hazel eyes. "And should you not be calling me 'Your Grace' now, Dick?"

Warwick glowered sourly. "Edward, *your Grace*..." he said pointedly. "We have been friends for years. I loved your father, God assoil him. You and I fled to Calais together with my own sire..."

Edward folded his hands and stared down at them, mood changing in the beat of a heart. "My uncle Salisbury, may he rest gentle in God's mercy! I am addled with drink and victory, Dick. Forgive me."

The Earl rose stiffly from his bench, gathering his cloak around him. "I too am weary after our battles. I ask leave to seek my bed."

"Granted." Edward nodded in Warwick's direction, and with a brow dark and troubled, the older man left the hall. Edward nudged Will Hastings, seated to his right, with his elbow. "Warwick seeks his bed. I, too, shall seek the comforts of the bedchamber. What do you think of that, Will?"

Hastings laughed and raised his goblet. "To the delights of the bedchamber, Ned! Long may they endure."

"He will never return, never," Eleanor Talbot murmured to herself. She was in the store-rooms below the hall, taking tallies of the cheeses and parcels of dried meat that stretched from floor to ceiling, exuding a pungent aroma. She had tried to throw herself into the duties of Lady of the Manor, delegating chores to the household, mediating squabbles between the servants, checking the rents from the village were paid, sending Steward Grene and a pack of carpenters to attend to the ramshackle cottages of the poorest in Great Dorset, which had grown nearly uninhabitable over the winter—and yet one thing was on her mind only. Edward

Plantagenet. Edward, who had won Towton and was undisputed King. Edward, who had expressed his desire for her, who had even spoken of *marriage*...

"It was all foolishness!" she suddenly cried out, losing track of her counting and throwing the tally stick onto the straw-strewn ground.

"My lady?" A stooped shadow darkened the arch of the door behind her. Agnes. "Is sommat wrong?"

Embarrassed, Eleanor scooped up the fallen tally stick. "No, not at all," she lied. "I was just counting and...and saw a mouse. I do not like mice."

"Is all in order, milady?" Agnes limped into the undercroft, peering at her mistress through the muggy gloom. "You sound vexed, upset. Is anything missing, do you think some of the local scallywags from the village have pocketed some goods from the delivery? I know some of those rascals are light-fingered..."

"No, no, nothing like that, Agnes. Nothing is wrong, *nothing*." At that moment, unexpectedly, her eyes began to fill with tears. They spilt down her cheeks, dripped from the end of her chin.

"My Lady—I knew sommat was amiss!" shrieked Agnes, throwing up her hands in dismay.

Eleanor thrust out a hand, preventing the maid from smothering her in an unasked-for embrace. "I...I am being foolish. You should not have seen my weakness. I will be fine in a moment."

"You should let yourself weep, if you'll pardon me saying so," said Agnes, clucking like a mother hen. "You've been through hard times, losing good Lord Thomas and your brother in those terrible battles."

Eleanor's face began to burn; she was glad the undercroft was dim, lit by a solitary, low-burning torch bracketed to the wall. Yes, she *should* be thinking of John and Thomas. Thomas her husband, dead not much more than a year, already a ghost in her memory. What did his voice even sound like? She could not remember....

But she remembered Edward's….
Remembered all too well.

That night she ate alone in her chamber, with only Blanchette for company. Agnes's old mother was ill so the maid had hurried off to the village to care for her. In silence, ringed by the light of a handful of tallow candles, Eleanor ate the pottage with rabbit and Manchet bread that cook had prepared for her. The bread and coney befitted Eleanor's status but it lacked the customary spices and the pottage was bland, mixed with a handful of turnips. Money had grown tight, what with repairs needed to the tenants' properties and to the manor house itself. Eleanor sighed, spooning some of the lacklustre stew into her mouth. A fox had taken some of the chickens and one of the best milk cows had sickened and died. Her horse needed shoeing, and the manor house roof needed a new repair. Glancing upwards, she noted the wet patch where rain had crept through a crack in the roof tiles. The dampness also crept along the walls, spoiling the faded remains of floral traceries that had delighted some long-dead lady hundreds of years ago. She was trying her best to make ends meet, but despite her best efforts, she was running out of money.

"What shall I do, Blanchette?" She spoke to the white greyhound, putting down her bowl on the rush-mat near her feet. Blanchette leapt from her bed, stretching her legs, and rapidly gobbled the remains of the meal before shoving her cold wet nose against her mistresses' hand as if trying to comfort. "I cannot manage much longer in this way. I must marry, and to be sure, the only man who's spoken of marriage to me will never come this way again. He's far too high and mighty now! I was a fool to even believe, for one mad, ridiculous second…"

Blanchette suddenly drew her head away from Eleanor's hand and stared towards the door. Her lips drew back from her teeth and she uttered a soft, menacing growl.

Hair prickled on the back of Eleanor's neck. She grasped hold of Blanchette's collar. "What is it, girl?" she said softly. "What do you hear?"

The dog growled again and tugged against her owner's hold.

"Hush!" chided Eleanor. "It is nothing. Probably just a rat within the walls!"

Blanchette let out a plaintive whine. Eleanor rose slowly. Who *was* here at the manor tonight? Agnes was in the village. Cook was usually abed by now. Steward Grene could be about his business, despite the lateness of the hour—it was probably he who made the noises that upset her hound. Eleanor's eyes narrowed; she had found Grene drunk a few times recently and was not terribly pleased by the standard of his service since Thomas's death. The security of the manor worried her, for there had been several robberies within the remote Burton hills, and the local sheriff would come only if there was a handsome purse to pay for his services. The bailiffs did their best but they resided in the village, which now seemed a hundred leagues from the manor house although, in reality, the first cottage with its neat vegetable plot was mere yards down the hill.

Releasing Blanchette's collar, Eleanor went to the window and unlocked the shutter. The aged, termite-eaten wood creaked on its hinge as she drew it open a crack and gazed out into the darkness, eyes straining to see if anything in the courtyard seemed amiss.

She saw nothing out of place—a loose hen pecking at the soil, the moon, hanging between shredded rags of cloud, shining dully on the bleached gold of hay piled in a wain propped against the outer wall. Although it had rained earlier, it was early June and the weather was warm; an eerie mist crawled from the ground as warm air met cold earth.

"It's nothing, Blanchette," she said to the Talbot hound, who, released from her hold, had scurried to the door and was sniffing at the draft wafting under it. "Nothing but a hungry old hen."

As if doubting her mistress, Blanchette's long pale ears went back and she released another throaty growl. Fur along the ridge of her back stood up stiff.

Eleanor had never seen the hound so distressed and it made her own unease grow. She leaned a bit farther out of the window, peering down towards the house gate. It was open. A bolt of anger shot through her. The steward, the stable boys—they had been careless of late; the great wooden gate with its stout latch had been left ajar several times recently. At one time, when Thomas was alive and more servants dwelt in the household, she had not worried about it overmuch—but with robbers in the nearby hills and unrest across the country in the last few months, she could no longer afford not to be vigilant.

However, open gate or no, she saw nothing amiss. Unfortunately, that did not mean she could relax. She had best investigate or her head would be filled with horrid fancies and she would toss and turn all night. Steward Grene would have to be roused, drunk or no, and she'd tell him to attend to his duties in a fitting manner—or leave in disgrace.

With a bristling Blanchette skulking at her heels, she left her bedchamber and walked down the unlit corridor to the hall. The central fire-pit, which was still used despite being rather unfashionable now, was filled by glowing embers that cast out a sullen light and made shadows race along the walls.

Blanchette gave another growl; Eleanor caught her collar again, keeping her from bounding away into the shadows. On the other side of the chamber, a figure moved, dark against the darkness.

"Wystan Grene, is that you?" she cried, peering into the gloom. It had to be the steward, but what on earth was he doing?

At that moment, the figure moved, sped towards her with frightening speed. A cloak billowed out, flapping like batwings; she could see no face. A gasp of fright tore from her lips and she let her fingers slip from Blanchette's collar.

"Call off your dog!"

She instantly knew the voice and shouted for Blanchette to come to heel. Unnerved by the strained shrillness of her mistress' command, the Talbot hound fell into a low crouch, tail between her legs.

"*Edward...*" Eleanor breathed.

The cloak fell away and there stood the King of England, dressed in dark travelling clothes with no badge, no jewelled collar, nothing to distinguish him other than his great height and comely visage, of course. "Have I surprised you, my lady?" he said with a certain impishness.

"I think my heart nearly stopped beating!" she said, and then her cheeks reddened and she fell to her knees. "Forgive me my lack of respectful greeting, your Grace."

He reached down and lifted her to her feet. She was a tall woman but he towered over her. He smelt of the summer, the warm woodlands, mixed with the fragrance of horse and a little sandalwood. "You need not kneel to me, Eleanor."

"Why...why are you here? And how did you get in?"

"The gate was wide open," said the King of England with a little laugh. "I thought you were waiting for me..."

"I...I was not." She was flustered, embarrassed. "My steward should have locked the gate; I was going out to do it myself. Where is the damn man?"

"Oh, my little party met him quickly enough," said Edward wryly. "He'd had a few flagons of ale, I deem, and came staggering out of the stable swinging a pitchfork at poor Hastings. We had to...take *care* of him."

Eleanor gasped and her hand flew to her mouth.

"Oh, fear not, he isn't dead. He will merely have a very sore head on the morrow."

"So, who is here with you? You have not travelled with a grand entourage."

"No, an entourage would not do for the business I am upon. It is only me, Will, Canon Stillington, the Archdeacon of Taunton, and three men at arms."

"A Canon?"

"Yes, of course; a man of God is needed…or have you forgotten?" Raising his hand to her face, he stroked his thumb down the outline of cheek and chin. "I gave my word to marry you. I meant it, and so I am here."

Drawing back, she shook her head in a daze. "I truly did not think…Surely this cannot be right. If you are to marry me, with you being who you are, your intentions should be proclaimed before the lords, in London…"

"Hush, my beautiful lady." He slid an arm around her waist and pulled her close to him. "We must do this now, here, in secret, this night. Consummate the marriage…"

She blushed to the roots of her hair.

"I know it is unorthodox but *circumstances* dictate the need. My father, God rest him, wished me to wed a foreign princess; my mother would have agreed. I must break the news of our marriage to her gently…"

"You think she will not approve of me?"

"You are a hero's daughter and of excellent blood, as good as her own, I deem. I am sure she will come around, eventually. Mother can be *bristly*…"

Eleanor stifled a nervous little laugh with her hand. "My mother can be like that too."

"There you go. Mothers…so alike. Not always easy to deal with." Edward drew her even closer, whispering in her ear, his breath warm against her skin. "You must tell no one. Threaten your servants, if you must…"

"I never threaten my servants; they are like friends!" she cried.

"You must this time…for us. Just for a short time, until it is safe to tell the world of our union. We cannot have certain parties finding out, like Dick Neville."

"My uncle," she said. "Why so, Edward?"

"Same situation as with mother. He helped me to the throne; I dare say he thinks he can broker a profitable marriage for me. But…" the King's face darkened, "I won't be told what to do, not by him, not by anyone. I shall make my own choices and be damned."

Eleanor wriggled away, just a little, uncomfortable with his intensity. "I…I have no fit garments to marry in. Not at this short notice."

Edward looked exasperated. "Woman and their vanity! I am sure your wardrobe does not contain a pile of rags."

"I have an old red velvet gown with gold beading. And pearls…"

"It will do. Anything you wear will look beautiful in my eyes."

"Edward, this is all happening too quickly…"

His eyes darkened; his hands dropped away from her. She saw his fists clench and suddenly felt a little fearful. He was not a man one would cross. "Do you no longer wish to marry me?"

"I…I…do, make no mistake, but…"

"Women! Always querying and fussing. Make haste! We do not have all the time in the world. Your people will doubtless be about before sun-up, and we cannot keep hitting your unfortunate steward on the pate to keep him quiet."

"Where? My chapel?"

The King nodded. "Safest that way! I have already sent Stillington there to wait for us. Now, go, ready yourself."

Gently he gave her a little push. She stood, knees wobbly, feeling as if she might fall…or faint. Blanchette, sensing something was amiss, let out a plaintive whine. Edward lunged forward to embrace Eleanor again, his good mood restored, as he kissed her neck, her cheek, her lips. "Hurry, woman, the night is getting old…and I, at least, am anxious to be abed soon."

Unsteadily she ran from the room, Blanchette bounding after her. Once in her bedchamber, she dragged on the lid of the brass-bound chest at the end of the bed. Her old red velvet gown, worn for a winter feast at Sudeley so long ago she'd forgotten the year, tumbled out into her hands, smelling faintly of dust and the dried lavender posies folded into it. She hoped it wouldn't fall apart at the seams…or be too tight a fit. Uncomfortably she wriggled out of her plain workaday gown and squeezed into the velvet dress. How on earth would she get it laced up at the back? She would look an utter fool. Maybe she *was* an utter fool….

All of the sudden, the chamber door flew open. Eleanor jumped in fright and Blanchette gave a sharp bark. Her heartbeat returned to normal as she saw a stunned-looking Agnes stumble in, home from the village. "Agnes, I had not expected you back so soon!" she cried shrilly, still wrestling with the gown.

"Mistress Eleanor, what is going on?" Agnes stumbled in her direction. "I got back and a man in the shadows of the gate grabbed me! I thought I was done for, I thought he'd ravish me and slit my throat! But then I saw 'im…that Lord Hastings, the friend of the young King, grinning through the darkness. He said I was to be sent to you but that I must be a good girl and keep my mouth shut…or else."

"I will explain…later," said Eleanor. "I'm glad you are here. I need to be dressed." She struck her hand against her velvet skirts, sending a light dust-cloud into the air. "Look at this, all full of dust! You must help me beat it out. And my best headdress, the butterfly headdress with the small red paste gems. Get that!"

"Are we having a feast? Is that what this is all about? But why so late; it's time for bed? Is young King Edward here?"

"Yes, he's here. Please, Agnes, ask me no more; this is as great a shock to me as it is to you."

Agnes fell silent and with trembling hands brushed down her mistress' skirts, laced her into the bodice of the gown and helped arrange her headdress. "What now, my Lady? Am I required further?"

Eleanor glanced around the room. "I am going to meet Edward…the King. While I am away, change my bed linen and get the fire blazing. Bring in wine, fruit. Then take Blanchette and go to the east wing. You may stay in one of the guest rooms there."

"You won't need me again later, to help you undress?"

Eleanor refused to meet her inquisitive gaze. "I...I will manage, Agnes. I have *business* to attend to tonight," she said hastily, full of embarrassment at her own feeble lie, but also feeling the first stirrings of deep excitement at what she was about to do.

She could see the dawning suspicion in Agnes' eyes. "By the Rood, Lady Eleanor..."

"No words, Agnes. None. What will be, will be. All I ask of you is that you keep your silence on the morrow...and every day thereafter. No tattling in the village."

"I swear it!" cried Agnes. "You can trust me, milady!"

"Good, now I must go. The King is waiting."

CHAPTER EIGHT

The chapel of Great Dorset manor was tiny, built at the house's first inception in the 1300's; most of the time Eleanor and her servants went to All Saints to pray, so the chapel had a cold, unused smell as Eleanor entered the low arch of the door. She had feared it would be in total darkness but when she arrived, she found the tiny room was lit by a spray of long *mensurae* candles—they were not hers, being of expensive make, so she assumed Edward must have brought them in his baggage.

The King was inside the chapel, lavishly dressed in a floor-length robe of midnight-blue cloth of gold. The entire outfit was decorated with golden sunbursts and around the edges of the sleeves were traceries of white roses. Hatless, his hair streamed in dark chestnut waves to his shoulders. He was like an angel in his masculine beauty, resembling the faint paintings of Gabriel at the Annunciation and Michael weighing souls that adorned the dank walls of the chapel below the faded figure of the Virgin Mary.

In front of Edward stood a man in priestly garb— Eleanor guessed that must be Canon Stillington. He had dark, slicked- back hair and a liverish complexion; he seemed nervous, licking his lips and shuffling from foot to foot. Lord Hastings was there too, bowing his head in her direction as she entered.

Edward beckoned to his friend. "Will, go and make sure no one enters the manor until well after dawn. Lady Eleanor, is there some sign we can give your servants to let you know that you have come to no harm, that all is as it should be with you?"

Is it as it should be? Nothing from this day will ever be the same again! Eleanor thought dazedly, but she nodded and removed a ring from her finger—a signet ring with a Marguerite, a daisy, engraved upon the bezel. It had been a gift from her mother Margaret upon her sixteenth birthday.

She handed it to Hastings with some reluctance. "Care for it well, my Lord Hastings. It is dear to me and I've worn it long. And tell any who may question, by that token they will know I am well and will address them when it is appropriate."

"I will guard it with my life," said Hastings with that air of mocking levity she found so irritating. She had no doubt, though, that he would do as he said to assist his friend.

Hastings slipped out the door; the sound of his footsteps grew faint in the corridors beyond.

Edward nodded toward the nervous Canon Stillington. "Now, Robert, let us waste no more time. We don't want a riot at the manor or a whole troupe of villagers trying to peer in the gate."

Stillington passed an arm across his forehead; sweat beaded on his brow despite the coolness of the dank little chapel. His mouth opened and shut a few times like a fish gasping for air.

Edward frowned. "Get on with it, man."

The Canon began to recite from the Bible; Eleanor tried to concentrate on the words, but they soon became an annoying buzz in her ears. Like the priest, she was awash with sweat, her head spinning. She was marrying the King of England, but not in glory in Westminster Abbey but in her own humble house. She wanted to pinch her own arm to see if she merely dreamed…

"Wilt thou have this man to thy wedded husband, to live together after God's ordinance, in the holy estate of matrimony? Wilt thou obey him, and serve him, love, honour, and keep him in sickness and in health? And forsaking all others keep thee only to him, so long as you both shall live?" She leapt in sudden fright as Canon Stillington addressed her.

Her tongue clove to the roof of her dry mouth but she managed to whisper. "I do."

Edward looked triumphant, glowing in muted glory at her side. "Edward Plantagenet, do you take Eleanor, daughter of John, late Earl of Shrewsbury to be your wedded wife, to have and to hold at bed and at board, for fairer for fouler, for better for worse, in sickness and in health, till death do us depart…"

"I do," said the King, his voice strong and firm. "And thereto I plight thee my troth."

Jesu, it was real. This was not a dream…

The King was slipping a ring onto her finger; it felt cold as ice. Canon Stillington was closing the Bible; the candles were wavering, descending into darkness, the faint wall paintings of Gabriel, Michael and Mary vanishing into the shadows as if they averted their faces from the unorthodox wedding. Then Edward was bending over her, his mouth seeking hers even as Stillington coughed nervously and toyed with the pectoral cross he wore.

Then Edward stepped back from his bride. "Come, Eleanor…my wife. Come, Stillington. Let the marriage bed be blessed and this union be made complete."

The newly-married couple exited the tiny chapel. Hastings was lounging outside the door in the shadows. "All quiet, Ned. As it should be."

"You must guide the way now, Eleanor."

"I hope all will be adequate for you, your Grace."

He let his gaze travel lingeringly up and down her form, as she shivered and not from the chill air seeping through the corridors of Great Dorset Manor. "I am sure it will be…more than adequate."

Wandering through the dim-lit halls, she guided the King of England to her bedchamber. The chamber where she had once lain with Thomas, the heir of Lord Sudeley, her first husband. The husband who had died for Lancaster and had now lost his widow to York. Stillington and Hastings walked behind them, in un-regal procession, Hastings holding a torch aloft to give them additional light.

"I wish I could have brought musicians," said Edward, glancing across at his pale-faced bride, "to play and make merry, but alas, secrecy took precedence. I had to leave them behind."

"It does not matter," whispered Eleanor, shaking her head. She thought back on her first marriage at Sudeley Castle; Lord and Lady Sudeley at the High Table, Lady Sudeley with a massive horned headdress; a Fool capering in particoloured hose making ribald jests; Thomas half in his cups as he was brought by his laughing friends to the bed of his shy, blushing sixteen-year-old bride high in one of the towers of the castle…

Here she was, no feast, no music, no Fool unless she *was* the Fool. Her wedding escort was a stuttering, nervous Canon and a grinning Baron who never seemed to leave the King's, her husband's, side. But no, she must not let her own nerves overwhelm her; she had named her price to Edward, had told him she would never be but a mistress. And he had cleaved to her will. Once consummation had taken place, there would be no doubt, not in the eyes of God or the eyes of man.

The door of her chamber loomed; never had it seemed so strange, so foreign, so ominous. She set her hand on the door-ring, turned it with a clatter of metal. Inside, the room was arranged in the manner she had advised Agnes; a fire burned, the bed linen was changed, the old, fraying carpets on the floor had been hastily beaten and brushed.

Stillington scuttled forward, reminding Eleanor of a spider in his rumpled dark vestments, and he flung Holy Water on the bed and muttered a hasty blessing with much emphasis on begetting and progeny. Once done, he made the sign of the Cross, then hastily exited, his feet pounding down the corridor and away.

Edward cast his arm around Will Hastings' shoulders, drawing him into a brotherly embrace. "Well, Will, do you wish me well?"

"Do you want me to undress you, Ned?"

"No!"

"How about your bride then?" Will pretended to make a lunge at Eleanor.

"Definitely not—you must remember she's not just any wench now! Now get out and go make yourself drunk." The King playfully swatted at his companion, who dodged his swinging fist and ran for the door, chortling with mirth.

"Good Night, Ned my King! I trust I will not see your face before midday."

"That's right, you won't!" yelled Edward. "Now shut that bloody door, will you?"

The door shut with a soft thud. Eleanor jumped, heart in her mouth. They were alone.

Husband and wife.

Once again past intruded on the present; she remembered her wedding night at Sudeley, in spring. Stars had dotted the firmament and the wedding party had moved across the lawns through the sumptuous gardens, singing and waving rushlights to chase away the gloom. Then, nigh on midnight, her ladies had whisked her away to the bridal chamber, removing her fine gown of virginal blue and her chemise of fresh, bleached linen, and tucking her naked into the bed, which was strewn with bouquets of newly-plucked flowers. Then Thomas arrived, dashing in his best finery, with young men who were close friends and companions, all merry-voiced and bawdy from Lord Sudeley's wine. They shouted ribald jests and began to pull Thomas's garments from him, making a silly game of it, while she had cringed in the bed, embarrassed, the counterpane dragged up to her nose. Then they were alone, awkward, fumbling, she innocent, he not much more knowledgeable but pretending to be a worldly man. In the end, after a brief and rather uncomfortable fumble, both ended up laughing nervously and holding hands beneath the covers, listening to the sound of crumhorns and tabor in the hall below where the revellers were whooping and clapping. "I didn't hurt you, did I?" Thomas had rolled on his side and asked her...and she had said nothing, just clasped his hand all the more tightly, and so their marriage began...And still, even though the memories of his words that night were clear, his face was just a blur, his voice unclear, as if he were underwater, lost to her—lost in time as the wonder and terror of the present overwhelmed her.

"My Lady." Edward's fingers caught hers, twined. His hand went up to her head, struggled with her headdress. He swore as it buckled and the veil caught round his arm and ripped away. Paste gems twinkled through the air like falling stars.

"It does not matter," said Eleanor.

"I will buy you a hundred more—far better ones," murmured Edward, throwing the ruined headdress to the ground.

He reached out, catching her shoulders and whirling her to face him. He was impossibly strong, his arms like iron bands as they encircled her waist. "Which shall it be then, wife? I undress you first or you undress me?"

She found she had lost the power of speech; he laughed that deep, easy laugh of his and lowered his head to hers, to claim her mouth in an impassioned kiss that took her breath away. A kiss that said *I have triumphed…you are mine!*

Deft fingers reached to the lacings on her gown; he was assured, practised; this was something he had done many times before, she could tell. Her gown flooded down, red as blood, foaming around her feet, leaving her only in her chemise. She felt near enough naked as the young King's gaze appraised her once more and was glad for the modesty afforded by her long black hair.

Edward's breath came heavily, noisily between his small, well-formed lips. He unlaced his long robe with its glimmering patterns of sunbursts and flung it away beyond the bed as if it were nothing of great value. Beneath he also wore a long, loose white linen shirt which he ripped over his head in a trice and hurled after his gown. Naked to the waist, he stood like a god in his tight hose, which showed the muscles of his long legs…and a straining codpiece laced with golden thread.

Eleanor could not help but look and Edward, all strutting male pride, ripped off the hose with surprising agility for one used to being undressed by squires and stood naked on the chill flagstones. "And now *you*, madam," he said, and without giving her chance to remove the rest of her garments, he reached out and took hold of the thin cloth, tearing it neck to hem. "I will buy you more chemises too," he murmured. "Ones made of silk, with ribbons. But for now…I will enjoy you without one."

Slowly he parted the veils of her thick, coiling hair, his fingers stroking the globes of her breasts, running over her flat belly to her thighs. "I have waited long for this," he breathed. "Even in my tent at Towton, facing death the next day, I dreamt of you, and how I would have you in the end. Christ, you make me burn, Eleanor—standing there clad in nought but your hair, as demure as a little nun…but I can see you tremble with anticipation, with desire, even as I do."

He caught her up and bore her to the bed, placing her down amongst the flower-petals Agnes had helpfully strewn. The headboard was carved with an image of Adam and Eve—with Eve handing her husband the fatal apple while the Serpent coiled around the bole of the Tree of Life.

"You were my forbidden fruit," said the King, covering her face and shoulders with kisses, teasing her nipples to hard points. She moaned and moved beneath his huge frame, circling his waist with her legs, drawing him closer. "But I am King…and nothing I want in my life will ever be forbidden me. Nothing."

Dawn arrived all too soon with the chattering of wakeful birds upon the roof. Eleanor awoke and heard the sound of daily life beginning outside the bedchamber window—almost as if nothing out of the ordinary had happened the night before. Wavering light filtered through the wooden shutters and flickered over the flagstones. Climbing from her bed, she reached over to her clothes chest and pulled on a chemise. Every muscle ached and her body tingled; her lips were swollen and bruised from the demands of the King's mouth; she touched them lightly with her finger, wondering. Never had it been so with Thomas; their perfunctory, although not unpleasant couplings, had primarily taken place to beget the heir that never came…Learned doctors said a man's seed would take hold with more surety if his wife too found pleasure in the act of love; if that was the case, she and Edward would soon have a fine brood of children…

Turning back towards the bed, she glanced at the King. Deeply asleep, he was sprawled out over the mattress, his long legs almost hanging off the end. His hair was splayed out around his head like a halo; his lashes lay dark on his cheeks; blue stubble coloured his strong Plantagenet chin. He looked very, very young, and Eleanor felt a sudden protectiveness towards him, her lover, her husband—but fear still needled her heart. What had they done? It was rash, impetuous—and dangerous. A secret marriage was frowned upon in general, and it would be even more scandalous with a King.

As if sensing her presence, Edward opened his eyes. "My Lady wife, to see you standing there with your hair loose and in disarray and just your chemise to hide your beauty, fills me with renewed desire…as I am sure you can see! Come back to bed, Eleanor, and lie with me again. I need you."

"I fear it is late, my lord…Edward," she said. "The sun is rising high in the sky. My servants fare abroad; I've heard them talking. Your men must have let them back in—which was wise. Even with my ring as a token of my good health, they might have panicked otherwise and called for the local sheriff, and that would have been a disaster."

"Indeed, it would have been." Edward sat up, tossed back his dishevelled locks, and swung his legs over the edge of the bed. "But Hastings is no fool, he would have seen them in before trouble started, and isn't your tiring-maid about? I saw her on my first visit to Dorset, a stout, red-cheeked woman. Walked with a limp."

"Yes, Agnes is here, she came back from the village early. I sent her to bed down on the other side of the manor…for our wedding night."

Edward's lip quirked. "I am sure I saw her peering out of a window when we sought the chapel."

"Agnes is *inquisitive*. I do not know how I shall tell her the truth."

"You won't." Edward's voice was low but held a note of firmness. Standing up, he dragged on his discarded robe, crumpled from where he'd flung it the night before.

"There will be questions!"

"I am sure there will be, but you must fend them off, Eleanor. For now. It will only be for a little while, I swear to you."

"So what must I expect?" Eleanor felt suddenly cold; she could not understand it, for it was June and the sun bright outside the windows.

"I will deal with things that need tending to—and then I will tell Warwick, my mother and the lords of the land that I have chosen a most noble and beautiful lady to be my Queen. They will be shocked, no doubt; Warwick will roar and mother might prove even worse than he, but they will both learn that what I desire shall be."

"How long might this take?" said Eleanor uneasily. She started twisting her unbound hair into a knot, not so much to tidy it but through nervousness.

He shrugged. "A few months perhaps? As soon as possible, I swear it. But as you can appreciate, after the last government under the old Mad King and his bitch, there is much that needs to be done to restore law and order and rebuild the country's stability."

"I understand," said Eleanor, although a queasy sensation knotted her belly. "I fear, though, that folk will think our union…an immoral one."

"And won't they be surprised when they find out we are wed!" said Edward. Stepping over to her, he showered kisses on her eyelids, cheeks and lips. "It is only for a short time, Eleanor. I know your honour is of great importance to you, but…!"

"I will survive." She forced a weak smile. "My honour may not, but one day the truth will be known."

"Of course it will." He gathered her close, a captive in his arms. "You are everything I've ever desired, Eleanor. I will make sure you are comfortable here. Remember how we mentioned the church roof in Great Dorset needed repairs? I will have it repaired. I…I will also have loaves of bread distributed to every villager in Dorset as I promised to do. Good quality bread."

"You are too kind," Eleanor murmured against his shoulder. Her hands pressed hard against his back, discerning the muscles developed by the use of sword and axe, the quiescent power of his warrior's frame.

"Now…" said Edward. "I know the sun is long up and I just put on my robe, but Christ, woman…the feel of you against me! Can we not go back to bed?"

CHAPTER NINE

He left within two days, waving cheerily as he departed the gates of Dorset manor, with Canon Stillington and Lord Hastings riding at his side and his small party of loyal guards ringed around him. Solemn-faced, Eleanor watched as the riders vanished into the distance, swallowed by the blue haze that hung over the Burton Hills.

"My Lady?" Agnes touched her arm. "Will you come away now? People are staring."

Eleanor felt an angry rebuke upon her tongue but schooled herself to calmness. It wasn't Agnes' fault. Naturally, her servants would be gossiping about what had transpired at the manor. She knew well there was tittle-tattle of how she had set aside her high morals to bed the handsome young Yorkist King. If only they knew the whole truth!

But she could not tell them.

Edward had told her not to and she dared not defy him. A woman should not defy her husband, let alone her King....

Sadly, she trailed back into the house and sat in the solar, a psalter open on her lap, although she found she could not read it; she couldn't concentrate on the words. Agnes joined her, sitting in silence for a while. Then, at last, the maid's breath rushed out in an explosion. "My Lady, forgive me, but what will you do now?"

"What do you mean, Agnes?" Eleanor laid the book down.

"About the King. What if there is a child?"

"You are forward, Agnes!" said Eleanor, angrier than she ever had been with her servant; who was, in truth, as close to a friend as she ever had. "I won't have it, do you understand?"

"It...it is only you I'm thinkin' of, my Lady. Left here, with a babby. Did he promise you he'd look after a child if there was one?"

"He promised many things, Agnes...but I can't tell you." Anger dying, she went to the maid and gave her a brief hug. "I am sorry I shouted—I was wrong. He will be back, Agnes...and it isn't as you think."

"I hope not, Lady," said Agnes, her round platter of a face creased with worry. "I truly hope not."

Edward IV was crowned upon June 28, mere days after Midsummer, when the sun blazed strongest in the sky and the days were long and hot. His Sunne in Splendour badge was blazoned all over London, pinned to the doublets of his followers and gleaming on the banners that streamed against the cerulean vault of heaven. Trumpets blared and the people of London rejoiced because the reign of the old Mad King was over and a Sun-King had taken his place, bright and beautiful, bringing in an age of new prosperity and joy. Edward had crushed his opposition at Towton; who could stand against him? Not Henry, cowering in the north with his wife; not even Jasper Tudor or the Earl of Oxford. The flower of the Lancastrian nobility lay mouldering on the field at Towton, where green gasses rose in clouds at night and started the locals spinning tales of the restless ghosts of fallen warriors.

Taller than any of his followers and attendants, Edward of York strode purposefully down the red ribbon of carpet leading into the interior of Westminster Abbey. He walked with great surety as if he had always known that to wear the crown was his destiny. He was God's chosen and he looked the part.

Pillars rose around him, trees of stone; the summer sun shone through the panes of painted glass high above, sending sprays of colourful light across the Cosmati tiles installed by Henry III. The large, raised rings that bore the tombs of the Kings reared up in splendour; shining dully, the gilt effigies of Edward's ancestors lay in repose—Henry III, who had rebuilt and refurbished the Abbey, Edward III, the flower of chivalry, with his streaming hair and peaceful face. Beyond them, however, before the high altar was Edward the Confessor's tomb, decked with gold and jewels, a place of pilgrimage and worship.

Edward knelt, the light from the windows illuminating his head. Undressed by his attendants, he was anointed with the Holy Chrism, the oil running hot on breast and back and shoulders and through his shining locks. Then he was dressed again in sumptuous robes of red velvet trimmed with kingly ermine, and Cardinal Bourchier set the crown upon his head.

Afterwards, at the lavish coronation banquet, Elizabeth Talbot danced with her husband John, the young Earl of Surrey. "Didn't the King look splendid?" she murmured. "What a day for England—for all of us. Mayhap all the terrible battles of the past will be over at last. I wish Eleanor could have seen the glories of this day; I wonder why she refused to attend? As my kinswoman, surely she would have been welcome."

Young John Mowbray did not know Eleanor well, having only spoken with her a few times when she had stayed at Framlingham. He was not much interested in his wife's kin; she had so many of them. "No doubt she is still in mourning for her husband, and it would have cost her much to travel to London. I cannot believe her income from her lands is very great."

"Oh, John, now you make me worry."

"She should think of wedding again—and soon. There must be many young nobles who would be interested. She's still young after all."

"You make her sound like a piece of property," said Elizabeth recklessly.

"I did not mean to. But I am realistic. If I were to die young, Bet…"

"Don't say such things!"

"I must! If I were to die, I'd want you to wed again…or go into a convent."

"I beg you let's not talk of such dire possibilities." She placed a finger to his lips, garnering a stare from the dancers milling about them. "It might court ill-fate."

Elizabeth and John continued to dance. Halfway through a stately pavane, the young Countess had the sensation she was being watched. She glanced over her shoulder to see the King standing nearby, watching her as she glided about the floor with her husband. It was more than impolite to meet the gaze of the monarch, it was forbidden; Elizabeth took a deep breath and pretended she had not noticed his stare. Her ears burned; she had met Edward before, briefly, at Framlingham, and had been warned that he was ever eager to have his way with ladies of beauty and distinction, no matter whether they were wives, widows or virgins.

The music ended in a wail of pipes. The dancers dispersed. Oddly flustered, Elizabeth excused herself and exited the hall to breathe the cooler air beyond.

Laughter wafted down the passageway. Above the torches trembled. She knew that laugh. It was the King. Her eyes darted about in the darkness; could she flee to the privy, hide herself away? No, there were others approaching through the hall, a troupe of entertainers ready to perform. She was trapped between the mummers and His Highness, the King, with his squires of the body milling about him.

At the end of the passage, she spotted King Edward's tall figure blacking out all light beyond. She dropped her head and fell into the deepest curtsey she could muster, praying he would pass by without noticing her.

He did not. She found herself staring down at two jewelled shoes, their pointed tips coated in silver. She dared not say anything, dared not even breathe.

"Countess de Warenne," said Edward mildly. "Rise."

Awkwardly she clambered up. "Your Grace."

"How like your sister you are, in many ways! I had not noticed before."

"You…you know Eleanor, your Grace?" asked Elizabeth in surprise. She remembered all too well how Eleanor had declined to stay at Framlingham for Christmas because Edward was likely to arrive.

"We have made…an acquaintance." Edward smiled to himself. "If you should see your sister or send a missive to her, I bid you tell her I wish her well and thank her for all her past hospitality."

"I certainly shall, your Grace."

"Good. My thanks, Countess." The King strolled away, surrounded by his favourites, leaving Elizabeth Talbot blinking after him in stunned surprise.

Later, whilst staying at a wayside inn on the long road home to Framlingham, Elizabeth turned to John and recounted what the King had said. "How could he have met my sister? She lives a simple life; she does not attend court. She stays on her own lands as you might expect from a widow-woman."

John's jaw grew tight; he would not look at his pretty young wife. "Her lands are in Warwickshire, are they not? No doubt he passed that way whilst travelling to and from fields of battle."

"Perhaps," said Eleanor, "but even if she provided lodgings for the King and some of his men, why would he speak of her as he did at Westminster after the Coronation?"

John shifted uncomfortably. "You must know of the King's reputation."

"Yes…*yes*…but not Eleanor; she would never submit to any man, not as a mistress, even if he were King of England. Not Eleanor. My sister is pious and chaste!"

"Kings can be very persuasive."

"You are wrong, John. I know it. And yet…"

"There is no other explanation," said John Mowbray quietly, "as far as I can see. But don't let it worry you, wife—

ofttimes, being a King's mistress can eventually garner a fitting husband for a woman."

"How unworthy of you, John!" said Elizabeth, genuinely flustered at the thought that Edward's interest in her sister might not be an innocent one. Once she was home, she would certainly send a letter to Great Dorset—and pray that Nel would confide her secrets to her.

The Countess Warenne's missive arrived by fast courier. Eleanor sat in her solar, reading with delight the elaborate account of Edward's coronation and the following banquet. "How I wish I could have been there," she breathed, and then, as sadness gripped her. "As his wife, I should have been." Her moment of melancholy lifted, however, as she read Bet's next words. *His Grace the King spoke of you. He wished you well. I do not know what to make of his familiarity and hope you will enlighten me, your sister....*

"Oh, Bet, I wish I could tell you." Eleanor threw Elizabeth's letter into the brazier and watched the edges curl and blacken. "I dare not reveal the truth, not until he tells me I may. But, my dearest sister, you don't know how much gladness your letter has brought. He remembers me, he spoke of me..."

Sighing, she walked to the window. Beyond the hills were parched, bleached by the July sun. Corn stood golden in the fields. Clouds bubbled up over the crenellations of the church tower; a summer storm was coming.

With frightening suddenness, the sky darkened and cracks of thunder shivered the air and made the old stones of the manor house tremble. Lightning forks speared the sky over the conical roof of the old watch-tower on the hills. Leaning in the window, the wind ripped Eleanor's headdress away and sent her dark hair tumbling from its pins. But she cared nothing for the tumult in the sky.

There was a greater tumult in her heart. When would the Sunne in Splendour emerge to quell the turmoil of the storm that raged within?

When would Edward announce that he had found his Queen?

The summer sun was indeed shining, hanging like burning eye over Great Dorset manor, when a messenger finally arrived from the King. The man was clad in grey wool, unremarkable, with no trappings of a royal messenger, but Eleanor guessed who sent him from the first and felt her heart skip a beat as if she were a silly young girl. Quickly she called her steward to admit the man and bring him to her solar where she could speak in private.

Sitting on a stool, trying to retain a calm demeanour, she gazed up at the dust-rimed youth who stood before her in his worn riding boots. "What is your name, sir, and your purpose?"

"Lady, I am from his Grace the King. My name is Martin…Martin Worrall. The King has sent a missive to you." Reaching into his leather jerkin, he pulled out a rolled-up parchment, and kneeling, handed it to her. "His Highness asks that you destroy it after you give me an answer, yea or nay."

With trembling fingers, she broke the red wax seal on the parchment and unrolled it, reading every word with care. Then she read it again. After she was done, she rolled it back up and threw it on the brazier as directed, watching as the wax, sizzling, ran like rivulets of crimson blood.

"My Lady?" said the courier, Martin. "What is your answer? His Grace wishes to know as soon as he might."

A little smile curved her lips; she blinked back tears which would be unseemly in the presence of a servant. "Go back to London, Martin Worrall. Tell his Grace…my answer is yes."

Two weeks later, Eleanor left Great Dorset surrounded by a small company of guards sent by Edward. Again, none of them wore obvious devices, but were well-armed and riding good horses. She rode alongside them in a litter with Agnes as her one companion from Great Dorset.

"I wish you'd tell me what this is all about, mistress," said the maid, sucking on a sweetmeat Eleanor had given her.

"I don't know the full of it myself, Agnes." Eleanor peered through the litter's curtain to the changing landscape beyond. "His Grace has summoned me to Wiltshire, of all places."

"Do they speak all funny in those benighted lands?" queried Agnes in concern. "Will I be able to understand what's going on?"

Eleanor laughed. "I am quite sure you will be fine, Agnes. It's not as if…as if they are Scots!"

"God forbid!" Agnes threw up her hands, horrified at the thought.

Eleanor did not know what they *would* face, however. When Edward's messenger arrived, she thought at first she was receiving a summons to London, where she would be proclaimed Queen. Instead, Edward asked that she meet him in Wiltshire, not in the main town of Salisbury, with its mighty cathedral founded long ago by the Countess Ela, but near Marlborough, which had a royal castle but one that was falling into decay.

The little entourage began to slow; the sounds of settlement—dogs barking, people calling out, bells clanging—became audible. Eleanor flicked the draperies aside again. In the distance, she saw an old-fashioned stone castle seated on a huge, upthrust earthen mound, and beyond it a bustling little town with a church adjacent to the castle gates and a series of shops lining a wide central street. The street ran up to a second, smaller church on the heights, with little lanes and crowded houses winding around it. "This must be Marlborough," she announced to a less-than-impressed Agnes.

The company passed onwards, giving Marlborough a wide berth. The countryside grew greener and hillier, with dark oak groves interspersed by patches of fertile farmland. Turning off the muddy road to a narrower track, they headed toward a stout rubble church with an ancient manor tucked in behind it. Gallows stood near the settlement on a hillock; mercifully the noose, swinging fitfully in the wind, was empty.

"Where is this place?" Eleanor called out to the lead rider, a man who'd introduced himself as Robert Welles. "And who is lord here?"

"We come to Wilcot, my Lady," replied Welles. "The manor and gallows tree you see belongs to the Prior of Bradenstoke. Soon our journey will be at an end and you can alight."

The entourage passed on until they reached another small hamlet, where the riders drew rein and the litter-bearers halted. Eleanor was handed down by Welles into the dusty yard of what appeared, to her eyes, to be a large and rather untidy farm.

"Where is this place?" she asked uneasily, eyeing the sprawl of buildings. Pigs were wallowing in a pen against one wall; farmhands were filing in and out of a rather ramshackle barn at the rear of what she assumed was the manor house.

"Draycott Fitzpayne, madam."

"And why have we stopped here?"

"Orders from his Grace the King," said Welles—a little sheepishly, Eleanor thought.

"Oh, my Lady, it is Awful!" Agnes opined, pressing her hands to her heart like a giddy maiden in a faint. "This cannot be right—I'm frightened! I'm sure we're about to get our throats slit!"

"Be quiet, Agnes!" Eleanor frowned at her maid. "You are not helping." Drawing herself to her full height, she faced

Robert Welles. "You must explain more clearly to me and Agnes."

"His Grace himself will explain all, my Lady. I can tell you nought save that he directed you be brought to the manor house of Draycott Fitzpayne."

"Manor House," Eleanor repeated dubiously, glancing over Welles' shoulder at the deteriorating building with its decayed timbers and crooked gables.

"We're to *stay* here?" shrilled Agnes, ignoring her mistress' earlier command of silence. "It's scarcely better than a hay-byre!"

The King's men were already unloading chests of Eleanor's goods from the baggage wain and hauling them towards the door of the rambling house. "I guess we are, Agnes," muttered Eleanor. "I do not think we have much choice in the matter."

Lifting her skirts out of the churned-up mud in the courtyard, she stepped briskly towards the manor house door, Agnes stumbling along at her heels, sputtering and shaking her head in dismay. "Lord help us!" the maid cried. "Look at those yokels by the pigpen staring at us!"

"Ignore them, Agnes. Hurry, let's get inside." She glanced at the sky where a threatening cloud hung, its hue as black as her mood had become. "It looks as if it will soon rain."

They entered the manor just as the heavens opened. Rain hammered on the roof, splashed across the muddy courtyard, struck and shuddered the windows with their slats of discoloured old glass. Walking through a narrow corridor that dog-legged this way and that, they entered the compact hall of the house. If Eleanor thought Dorset was in poor repair, this was far worse, the flagstone floor bare, the walls bleak, the windows high and antique, allowing in but little light. No modern fireplaces warmed the place and even the old-fashioned firepit was inadequate, filled to the brim with ashes and bits of bone from former meals. A sullen red glow emerged from its heart; an ancient crone was jabbing it with a metal poker.

Realising Eleanor and Agnes had entered the room, the old woman jumped back, dropping the poker with a clang. "My Lady, forgive me, we did not think you would be arriving so soon."

"I did not know I would be arriving at all," said Eleanor. The woman stared blankly; she had watery eyes and no teeth. She looked as old as God Himself.

"Who is master here?" asked Eleanor with irritation.

The woman looked surprised. "You...*you* are, my Lady."

"Me?" Eleanor frowned. "I do not understand."

"It's what the messenger told us. A messenger from his Grace—the new young King. My name is Wilmot...Wilmot Adams. I have lived in these parts nigh on three score years and ten—the lifetime of a man according to the Holy Bible!"

"Well, Mistress Adams, your words are a surprise to me. Who was here before me?"

"Mistress Skillings. Married into the Waytes of Southampton, another local lot, with pretty daughters; the family is up the vale now, farming other lands. Drayton wasn't profitable enough, my Lady, so Master Wayte sold it. There were only ever seven tenants at any time; this isn't a wealthy place, I'm afraid. The current tenants live in the outbuildings you may have seen on your way in."

Eleanor could find no more words; a great weariness and despair fell over her. She had travelled miles expecting to see Edward, perhaps to be brought as his queen to the royal castle of Marlborough—and she was here instead, seemingly the owner of a run-down manor in the middle of nowhere. Above her head, the rain continued to lash the roof; water began to leak through worm-eaten slats and trickle down the walls. Agnes made a low moan.

"I have journeyed long, Wilmot," said Eleanor, with a tired sigh. "I presume my accommodation is ready?"

"Oh, yes, my Lady," said old Wilmot, nodding. "I beg you come with me!"

She led Eleanor and Agnes through the hall and up a narrow stone staircase comprised of but four worn steps. Then they stood on a landing which led into a tiny solar with a screened off section for sleeping. Eleanor's goods had already been deposited haphazardly around the room. The place smelt damp but the brazier here was burning and bags of dried herbs offset any offending scents.

Eleanor inspected the bed. A canopy stretched over it, to keep off bugs that might drop from the ceiling, but she was surprised, after witnessing the decay in the rest of the farmhouse, to see that the canopy was full of rich silver thread. The stitching formed a massive rose. Tearing her gaze away, she stared down at the bed itself. Pure white linens, bleached and clean; blue silk broidered with golden falcons.

"Did the King..." she breathed, reaching out with a hand to stroke the silk.

Old Wilmot smiled a toothless smile. "None other, my Lady."

Agnes began poking about the chamber, closing the warped window-shutters against draughts, testing the furnishing for dust with an accusing finger. Suddenly she stopped, placing her hands on her broad hips. "Where am I to sleep. There's a bed for my Lady, but not even a pallet set out for me!"

"You will only be required when her ladyship calls." Wilmot fixed Agnes with a bleary-eyed stare. "You are to have a small room adjacent to this chamber; I will show you…."

"No…*no*!" interjected Agnes, waving her hands in agitation. "I am not leaving Lady Eleanor's side whilst we are living in this…this place. I am sworn to protect her in all circumstances."

Wilmot smirked and gave a little laugh, disguising it with a phlegmy cough. "Oh, don't you worry, my girl. No harm will come to your mistress under this roof. She's under his Grace's protection…"

Agnes looked as though she might weep. "Oh, Lady Eleanor, I don't like any of this tomfoolery! I know it's not my place to say anything but I'm so worried about what you've got into here!"

"Agnes, Agnes." Eleanor caught the maid's hands in her own; they were shaking. "I cannot tell you everything that's happened the past few months, and what I expect you imagine has gone on is not quite the truth. But if the King is coming here, we will be safe, both of us. Do as Wilmot says; your quarters are just next door."

With hang-dog face, Agnes followed the still-smirking Wilmot into the corridor beyond the solar. The door shut with a bang. Eleanor removed her simple travelling wimple and loosed her hair, then sat on the bed with a huge sigh of relief. Every bone in her body ached and soon she found herself falling back on the coverlet with its golden falcons. Vaguely she was aware of the door opening and Agnes and Wilmot having words about who would cover her up against the cold and who would bring food for when she awoke. It turned out Agnes won the first, pulling a sheepskin from a chest to tuck around her, and Wilmot won the right to the second, creeping in on unsteady feet with a carafe of wine in one hand and a pottery bowl filled with pottage in the other. She put them down on a stand and shuffled away.

Eleanor slept fitfully. When she awoke, darkness had fallen outside. No strips of evening light reached through the shutters. Groggily, she arose and laved her face in a brass basin near the bed and took a most unladylike swig of the wine Wilmot had left. Outside silence reigned; the rain had stopped. Reaching for the left window shutter, she pulled it open; the room, the single taper on the sideboard unlit, was too dark, too oppressive. Cold air flooded into the chamber.

Beyond the farm, the sky was ebony, the stars hard and watchful eyes. The clouds had rolled away, revealing a thin, finger-nail paring moon; its wan blueish light shone on rows of low hills topped by ancient mounds and ridges like crowns on the head of slumbering giants. Somewhere a fox yelped, its voice an almost human scream that lanced through the silence. Eleanor crossed herself. A landscape of dark dreams, that could fill the head with wild fancies.

Suddenly she heard the sound of singing carried on the chill breeze. Down the nearby lane trotted several horses, bridles jingling, the foremost of the riders holding up torches to light the way. Fog-trails from the damp ground wafted around them and for a moment, caught in the golden nimbus of the torches, she thought she witnessed the Faerie Ride, the procession of the ever-living Lordly Folk too wicked for heaven but too good for hell, whom the countryfolk said fared out from old burial mounds to capture human brides... She crossed herself again and then suddenly her heart leapt with a mingling of both fear and longing, and she laughed out loud.

It was Edward riding down the lane towards the manor of Draycott Fitzpayne surrounded by a small party of followers. *He* was the King of the Otherworld, tall and imposing on his white horse, his hood thrown back and the flames around him rippling on his flowing hair.

Even as she stood in the window, watching, he glanced up from the lane and saw her. With a grin, he spurred his horse towards the manor house door, leaping from the beast's back with the agility of an athlete and leaving the reigns dangling.

Flustered, Eleanor retreated from the window. After her earlier journey, she looked unkempt, unattractive. How could she ready herself for the presence of the King, her husband? She began to bang on the wall, calling desperately for Agnes to attend her.

It was too late. The stablehands outside had taken the newcomers' horses and the front door banged open with a careless crash. Still in high spirits, Edward's companions continued to sing; distantly she caught some bawdy lyrics about a priest cuckolding the local lord with his 'fair young wyffe' who had gone to the church seeking guidance. She cringed.

Then footsteps thundered on the stairs and into the solar barged the King, his cheeks ruddy from the cold and his eyes hot. Almost at the same time, Agnes, having been summoned by her mistress' cry, almost collided with his back. She gave a terrified squeal, tried to stop herself from touching the King's royal person, and fell flat on her well-padded rump.

Edward turned slowly to blink down at her. She cowered, moaning with fear as he leant over her fallen body. "Up you get, good dame," he said with mock courtesy, extending his hand. "I trust you haven't hurt your…ah…your…"

Agnes took his hand, scarlet-faced as he pulled her to her feet. "Um, no, your Grace…Thank you, I was just…Lady Eleanor…"

"My Lady will have no need of you till the morning. I will take care of her." Agnes danced around in embarrassment while Edward savoured every moment of her discomfort. "Off you go now, and no listening at the door!"

Agnes let out a gasp half of horror, half of indignation, and fled.

Edward kicked the door shut and turned. "So…is there no warm welcome from my wife?"

Eleanor hesitated for a brief instant then flung herself into his arms. He kissed and embraced her, his fingers struggling with the knots on her kirtle. "Christ, my fingers are too cold to function. I assure you the rest of me is not, however! I burn for you, oh God, I burn. As I rode down the lane, I saw you at the window, your hair like a dark curtain, the moon shining on your face and…"

"Edward…husband…" Eleanor disentangled herself from his embrace as gently as she could, although she trembled with both nerves—and longing. "First, before anything else transpires, we must talk…"

"Talk. Talk!" Edward's visage grew similar to that of a sulky child; he folded his arms defensively. "I have ridden to you after months spent away from your side, and you wish to talk? Bah, and I can imagine there is nought good in your words, unless..." His face brightened and he stared hard at her slender midriff. "You are not with child, are you?"

She shook her head; quivered inside as she saw his expression grow sulky once more. "No, alas, I am not. It is not God's will, not yet. Perhaps when I have finally been proclaimed as your wedded wife and we spend more time together."

He slumped down on the edge of the bed, a moody giant. "So that's what this is about. The time is not right yet, Eleanor, I told you before."

"It's been some months…"

"Do not question me!" She jumped back at the sharpness of his voice, felt tears spring to her eyes. She raised her hands to cover her face.

The King softened. "Oh come, do not cry. We are together, we have much to celebrate."

"I do not even know why I am here!" Eleanor's voice trembled. "When I first received word from you, I thought you would lead me into Marlborough with the bells ringing. Instead, I was taken to this…this farm in the middle of nowhere."

"*You*r farm now," said Edward, "and all of Draycott Fitzpayne, Oare Under Savernake, and, a little further afield, Colcutt and Chicklade Ridge. You shall receive all the rents from these properties and it will help maintain you at Great Dorset. I have the necessary documentation ready, but as with our marriage, my gift—call it a late wedding gift—must remain a secret between us. If any ask, you must say you purchased the lands yourself."

Agitated, she shook her head. "I cannot tell such lies, Edward. No one would believe them! I do not have spare money to purchase distant lands. I am not a rich heiress."

"No, *ungrateful* is what you are!" Edward said, petulant, his eyes narrowed.

Eleanor sank to her knees before his booted feet. "My lord King, please do not be angry. I beg you understand my fears."

"And you must understand mine! I fear to alienate certain lords, like your uncle of Warwick, should I say I have chosen my own bride without their help." He raised her up, drew her onto his knee, nuzzled the white stem of her neck. "Now, come, give me proper greeting as a wife should."

"But when shall it be? When?"

"I cannot say. The business of ruling is a difficult one; I have had much on my mind. You, too, have been on my mind, naturally, every day…and every night. But for now, our marriage must remain a firm secret."

She did not know what to say and buried her face upon his shoulder, hiding the disappointment and worry in her eyes. "Blow out the candle." Edward nodded towards the taper on the sideboard. "I am cold from my ride. I do not want further coldness from my wife."

She clambered up, dishevelled, and blew out the taper. The room fell into darkness save for a patch of moonlight dappling the rush-mat on the floor. Rats skittered in the walls; a white tail of candle smoke hung in the gloom like the finger of a spectre.

Eleanor climbed into the bed, with its silken cover adorned by falcons, and into the ardent embrace of her husband, the King.

The King who had not and would not yet acknowledge her, his wedded wife, as Queen.

Edward stayed for five days, and in those days Eleanor was his world. He took her out riding across the wild and dramatic landscape, hunting with her in Savernake Forest, galloping along the ridge of the ancient Wansdyke, showing her the sunlit beauty of Martinsell Hill, Golden Ball, and Walkers Hill. At the latter, they halted and Edward raised a hand to shield his eyes from the sun as he gazed upwards. "Look, Eleanor, what do you see?"

Eleanor squinted. Dark against the bright background of the sky, she spotted the hump of a long, low mound high upon the height, its presence as commanding as that of a castle. Several tumbled stones lay embedded in its bank. A hawk circled it, screaming; it dived for some mole or vole in the grass and disappeared. Eleanor shuddered; this seemed a lonely spot, out of time.

Edward was still looking at her, waiting for an answer. "I do not know," she said honestly, "but it feels *strange* here. As if time has ceased. Maybe it is haunted." She crossed herself.

"The locals call the hillock Woden's Grave," said Edward. "He was a god of pagan times. They say there was a battle on these heights long ago."

"I do not want to think of battles," murmur Eleanor, suppressing a shudder. Above the ancient grave mound, the hawk reappeared, dipping and diving, its harsh voice ringing out over the bald hilltops. "Edward, please tell me the battles are all over."

Edward's fingers tightened on the reins of his destrier. "I cannot promise such a thing. Henry still lives, and his son. If they remain in exile, let them live in peace but if they should return..." He shrugged. "Now you know why I dare not bring you to court. It is important that I make England secure, make my *throne* secure. Your own safety would only then be assured."

"You think I am not safe?"

"You are not, as there are still those who love me not but serve the cause of Lancaster, even in secret. What would they do if they found out you were my wife?"

She drew her cloak more tightly about her; the wind, shrilling down from the heights, felt unseasonably cold—it rushed through the long grasses, sent clouds bundling up behind the head of the hill. A happy day darkened. The first spots of rain began to darken the soil beneath their horses' hooves. "If I were at your side," she murmured. "At Westminster…"

The rain fell harder, the wind throwing it into both their faces. Edward rubbed a velvet sleeve across his eyes, dashing away droplets of water. The jewels of his hat brooch danced beneath a sheen of wetness. "Come, it is time to return to Drayton Fitzpayne."

Something had soured Edward's mood; Eleanor could only assume he had received unpleasant news from his ministers and advisers in London. He grew pensive and dissatisfied, stalking about the farmhouse at Drayton, while the over-awed servants stood frozen like statues, afraid of causing offence.

At length, he shook his great head as if awakening from a dream. He clasped Eleanor's hand. "It is time for you to go, alas."

"Go! But my lord, is this not my house now?"

"Yes," he said, but his smile was not particularly warm, "by my good graces, of course. I have duties to attend to, you understand. I think you would be best back at Great Dorset, where you are known and loved…"

"Edward…" She reached out to him. "If we must part, let it not be so soon."

"I thought you were scornful of this place." He nodded toward the damp wall, with its bubbling plaster and patches of mould. "Now suddenly, you wish to stay."

"Because you are here," she said, "my husband whom I love and honour above all things."

He kissed her on either cheek; she pressed against him, longing for him to claim her mouth with his own. To kiss her cheek seemed the gesture of a man to a sister, a mother. Not a wife.

"You are a sweet, good woman, Eleanor," he said, but no lingering farewell kiss was forthcoming. "Tomorrow, a chariot will arrive to bear you back to Great Dorset."

Eleanor shed no tears as she climbed into the carriage with Agnes. Edward did not come out into the courtyard for her departure. "Where is he, then?" asked Agnes, rather disrespectfully.

"Be calm, Agnes, it would not be fitting."

"Fitting," said the maid with scorn. "Oh well, at least we shall, God willing, make it back to dear Dorset without having our throats slit by some Wiltshire brigand."

Silent, Eleanor sat down upon her cushioned seat. The chariot, surrounded by its small company of guards, began to roll down the lane. Through a crack in the curtains, she saw the farmyard and the higgledy-piggledy manor with its buildings of various styles and ages vanishing in the distance. Vanishing, with Edward inside.

A cold, sick feeling clawed her innards. *You have been deceived,* a voice whispered in her head, a mocking voice...her own voice, but full of derision and rage at herself. *You let lust consume you, lust and desire. Satan moved your tongue to say 'Aye' and made you spread your legs...*

"But it's not a sin, we are wed!" she suddenly cried in agony, as tears burst from her eyes and streaked down her cheeks.

Agnes gave a gasp and froze, startled into silence for once. She dared ask no questions, merely thrust a kerchief into Eleanor's hand with which to dry her tears.

The chariot rumbled onwards, wheels grinding on the rutted road as it headed north towards Warwickshire.

The King entered the Great Hall at Marlborough Castle, magnificent in his ermine robes and cloth of gold. He beckoned to Lord Hastings with impatience. "Well, Will, where is she? I thought she'd be here."

"The minx is waiting to make a grand entrance, I'll wager, Ned," said Hastings. "She's more than proud, that one."

"That's not all she is." Edward gave his friend a knowing grin as he sat down in his chair of estate beneath a canopy painted with stars and suns.

At the entrance into the hall, there was a sudden flurry of activity, a parting of the guards and courtiers and pretty courtesans that flocked wherever royalty lingered.

Bold as brass, a woman strode into the chamber and dropped a deep curtsey before Edward's seat. Young, her lips were painted cherry-ride; her stylish gown matched their colour. Her brows had been neatly plucked, her forehead shaved until it gleamed like a white pearl, and on her head towered a great conical headdress wreathed in violet veils that shimmered as she walked. About a swan-like neck gleamed a pale gold necklace with a pendant that was a White Rose.

Edward felt pleasure as he saw it, glimmering coldly in the hollow of her throat; he had given it to her.

"My lord King!" she said in a melodious voice, rich as honey. It made the young monarch shiver with anticipated pleasure.

"Mistress Elizabeth Wayte," he said. "What brings you here from Southampton?"

"Many pressing matters, your Grace!" the girl said. "My father Thomas Wayte was taken ill when attending to his Wiltshire properties. I came to make certain he was well, as a good daughter should."

The corner of Edward's mouth twitched. "Most commendable, mistress Wayte. I take it, he is recovered?"

"Yes, yes," she said, almost dismissively. "It was just a griping of the bowels and nothing a good posset could not cure. He's fully recovered and riding in a carriage back to Southampton even as we speak."

"And you need come to Marlborough to tell me about your father's watery bowels?"

"No, your Grace. I come on another mission. One far more important." Her innate confidence suddenly seemed to waver; in fact, so did she. The girl's visage paled and she looked as if she might faint.

"You...make sure the lady does not fall!" Edward shouted at the Esquires of the Body clustered around his High Seat.

One of them reached the young woman, steadying her with a hand. She seemed to recover her equilibrium quickly, although her face remained chalk-white beneath her henin.

"Are you ill, Mistress Wayte?" asked the King with some concern. "Are you afflicted as your sire was?"

A hushed murmur ran through the chamber. All feared pestilence and unknown sickness—the shadow of last century's Black Plague still hung over England.

"For all it may look, I am well," said Elizabeth Wayte, and again fierceness entered her tone. "But I must speak with you, your Grace. Alone."

Now Edward looked both intrigued and slightly alarmed. He crooked his finger at a page. "Take Mistress Wayte to my private closet, boy. I will be along in a while when I have heard all complaints and supplications from the citizens of Marlborough."

When the King had finished his duties in the Great Hall, he retired to his private closet, dismissing the squires, who ran sniggering down the dark stone corridor. They would be soundly beaten if caught laughing at the King's affairs but that only made their disrespect somehow more appealing— the hint of danger, the threat of the birch. They also knew their master well and since they were not so many years younger than the new monarch, there was a hint of jealous and juvenile sport in their mirth—if *only* they were as successful with women as King Edward! The King had dozens of wenches under his belt already, surely, while most of the squires had not even yet tupped a lusty dairymaid or visited the Stews!

Edward entered the small, enclosed room with its dark wood panels—a recent addition—and tapestries of Biblical scenes. Elizabeth Wayte was waiting, her graceful swan's neck gleaming in the candlelight, the little White Rose at her throat moving with every breath. As Edward approached, she curtseyed, and when the King gestured for her to rise, she did so at once but with an almost arrogant air.

"Will you sit, mistress?" He gestured to a window embrasure, plumped with velvet pillows.

Lifting her skirts, she sat daintily upon the pillows and Edward sat down beside her. His hand came to rest on her lap, full of familiarity. "What is it, Eliza?" he asked, all formalities dropped. "Why are you really here?"

She shifted uncomfortably. "My father was *truly* ill, it was not a lie."

"But…?"

"While I tended him, he let me know of the lands recently purchased in Oare and Draycott Fitzpayne."

"How does that in any way concern you, Eliza?"

"I know you gave them to a woman—and that she was at the farmhouse with you."

"Oh, you jealous little cat," said Edward with a mocking grin.

"I have not seen you for months, Ned…your Grace," pouted Elizabeth Wayte. "I fear you are losing interesting in me, and it fills me with sorrow…"

"How could I lose interest in such a fiery little beauty?" Edward reached out and removed her headdress. Long coils of golden red hair tumbled over her shoulders.

She stood up and impulsively grasped his hands, bringing them up to press against her round, high breasts. "Would you miss this, my lord King? Would you indeed?"

"Oh, I would!" he laughed throatily. "Christ, I wish the top halves of women's garments were not nigh as impregnable as armour!"

"That may be so," she said, "but the lower half is not so armoured." Grasping her skirts, she pulled them up near the tops of her thighs. "There…what you have always loved. Is that other doxy of yours as fair as I? The one you had at the farmhouse? I heard she is dark and ugly."

Edward shifted himself yanking at his clothing as he pulled her down on top of him amidst the cushions in the window embrasure. "No, she is very fair. Fair and honourable and virtuous."

"Am I not so endowed?"

"Oh, you are beautifully *endowed* in every way, my sweet leman." His hand slipped between her thighs, drawing a gasp from her painted lips. "But virtuous, you are not. I do not believe either that you have travelled from your home in Southampton just to wipe an old man's arse and then chide your King about having another mistress."

"You are right, Ned." She wriggled away from him, drawing herself half upright, dishevelled but beautiful. "There is another reason."

"And what is that reason, Eliza?" He reached for her again, pulling her close to feel the urgency of his need.

"I am with child."

Edward stopped what he was doing, an expression of surprise on his face. Then he gently pushed her aside and sat up. "These are good tidings, Eliza. Good indeed! I will see that the child is fed, clothed and schooled."

"You are not angry then?"

"No, I am pleased! My first bastard, by God! My son!"

"What if the child's a girl?"

"Well, she will be a beautiful girl, without a doubt—and when she's old enough, I'll find her a rich husband. I'll do the same for you, too, Eliza; a King's concubine is always a prize catch, especially when she's shown her worth by producing a babe or two."

Her news delivered and the response positive, Eliza resumed her seductiveness towards her royal lover, lying back on the seat with her red-gold hair flooding down and her back arched. "So…you won't spurn me for the dark wench?"

"No, never, little sweetling." Edward shook his head. "Of all the women who I've lain with, you are the cleverest, the wiliest. I like that, Eliza Wayte. I like that."

Eleanor spent the rest of the year working hard on her estate at Great Dorset and also attending to her other Warwickshire manor of Fenny Drayton. It gave her the chance to thrust Edward from her mind, even though it was a grant from the privy purse that went towards the restoration of Dorset's church.

She was convinced, by the time winter rolled around, that she would not see the King again. She had been gulled and although their marriage was a true one, sanctified by a priest and consummated, Edward had clearly tried to buy her off with the Wiltshire lands—there was no other reason for him to give them to her. If she had ever dreamt of a crown, that dream was long dead. It would never be.

Agnes wandered after her mistress like a lost sheep, trying to engage her in conversation, for Eleanor's mood had changed since their dismissal from Draycott Fitzpayne. She smiled less and worked more, and spent more time on her knees in prayer in the chapel or the little church on the hill. "You mustn't take on so, my Lady," she said. "The King just did what Kings do...Well, what most men do, if given the chance. You're young, of good breeding and fair of face. You can find yourself a suitable husband."

Eleanor kicked at a sludgy ball of hay and dung that lay in the cobbled courtyard. "No, Agnes, that is exactly what I cannot do now, even were it my deepest wish."

Agnes was afraid to ask more, remembering her mistress' strange, unseemly outburst when they had left Drayton Fitzpayne for home. Eleanor was secretive and sorrowful, but Agnes was only a servant and dared not pry into her affairs. She wondered what would happen and secretly prayed that some nice young lord would pass by and show an interest in her mistress that would be reciprocated.

In November of that year, the sickly old Duke of Norfolk died and Eleanor's sister and brother-in-law became Duchess and Duke of Norfolk. John was still a minor, only seventeen, but John's family and advisers gathered round to aid the new Duke and his Duchess in their new roles

"I wish I could go to Bet," murmured Eleanor. "My mother yet lives, but it is Elizabeth who was always closest to my heart."

"Well, why don't you?" said Agnes stoutly. "You know she would appreciate your presence. And you never know who you might meet…"

"Enough of *that*; I would rather meet with no one!" Eleanor pursed her lips in disapproval. "But I will think of going to Framlingham, if I am wanted."

That night Eleanor wrote a hasty letter to Bet. *Sister, sorrowful am I to hear the Duke, John the Elder, has passed into God's care. I would be near to you in this time of sorrow and maybe for all time, for my sorrows and travails are great too. I cannot write of it, but may tell you with my own lips when we meet again… Your loving sister, E.*

The letter was never sent. The very next day a messenger arrived from the south, alone. Eleanor felt her belly clench up the moment she saw him. News from the King, she knew it. Sure enough, the courier passed her a document informing her that Edward would pass by Dorset soon while travelling to Warwick. Eleanor should expect his royal presence within a fortnight.

"Are you happy at these tidings, my Lady?" Agnes frowned in consternation as she grasped at Eleanor's sleeve. "You…you don't look terribly pleased." Eleanor was sitting at her embroidery, but her needle darned the air. A frown creased her white forehead.

"I am, of course I am, but…" she heaved a great sigh, "I do not wish to continue in this manner. Secret meetings. A day here, a day there. It is not right. It is not *fair*…"

"No, it is not, but no one here will hold it against you, Lady. No one does. You can go on, as I've said before. At least he didn't leave you with a child."

Eleanor shuddered and suddenly hugged herself. Her needle fell tinkling to the floor. Blanchette padded up and sniffed at it, then lay her head against Eleanor's knee as if in commiseration. "A child…No, Agnes, maybe a child would have saved everything. Maybe. Now…" She jumped from her stool, sending her embroidery flying like a sail and frightening the hound, who shied away, ears back in fright. "Once again we must prepare for the King's arrival. But I swear to you, it will not be as before. He will not fly in and out of here as the wind sweeps down from the hills with hardly an afterthought. I have plans. I know what Edward wants of me…but, this time, I will state what I want from him too. One thing I dare say he will never give me, although it was sworn, but I may wrangle other gifts which will bring solace to those I care for. That, at least, will bring me some comfort."

The King looked pleased; he lifted Eleanor's hand to his mouth, his hair falling in chestnut-gold strands around his face. "You smile," he said. "I am glad to see you merrier. It was never my intention to bring you unhappiness."

"I know," she said, "and I have accepted my lot. You still are not ready to bring me to court, are you, my…husband."

His glance slid from her face. "No, I told you before."

"Too much unrest."

"Yes."

"And Uncle Warwick and your mother might be shocked."

Edward dropped Eleanor's hand and folded his arms over his chest, a scowl darkening his pleasant visage. "There is a certain tone in your voice, madam…"

"Forgive me, husband." Lightly she kissed the end of his chin. How beautiful he was and how her heart was breaking but she knew the truth—the King did not love her. He had tricked her into his bed, and while the ceremony in the chapel was real, who was there to verify it? Edward's friend, Lord Hastings. Canon Stillington who was clearly in his master's pocket. They would never speak out against Edward. She'd be mocked as a madwoman if she came forward with her claim, and it would bring her not Edward's love but eternal enmity. He was not a man one would wish to have as an enemy.

"I must ask you though, my lord King, a boon." She sank to her knees, her skirt prettily arranged around her, her hand on Edward's knee.

"What is it?" His eyes narrowed suspiciously.

"What I ask is not for me," she replied, "but for one close to me."

"Speak," said Edward.

"My request is for Lord Sudeley, my former father-by - marriage."

"The old Lancastrian. The one who was a banner bearer for Mad Harry Six. What does *he* need?"

"He was always kind to me, Edward, even after Thomas was killed. Of late, though, his health is not good. He fears a summons to attend parliament in London. He has gout and walks with a cane…"

"Enough!" Edward raised a hand for silence. "I have heard enough."

"My lord husband?" Eleanor glanced up hopefully.

"I will grant Lord Sudeley leave to remain at his castle. There's no fool like an old fool, particularly a Lancastrian one—and I need new men around my throne, not those stuck in the ways of the old regime."

"You are too gracious, my dearest lord." Eleanor raised her hand as if in supplication. "But I have one more thing to ask, on his behalf. His doctors have said he needs more rich meat…"

Edward's eyebrows lifted. "You are asking me to *feed* Lord Sudeley?"

"Of course not, my Lord. But in his old age, he can no longer hunt, which used to give him such pleasure. The occasional buck from the royal forests would gladden his heart and ensure his loyalty to you."

"So, you suggest I obtain Ralph Boteler's loyalty through his belly," grumbled Edward.

"No, not really. Overall, it is just a kindness to an old man who was good to me. Your wife."

Edward sat in silence for a moment, deep in thought. Eleanor rose with grace and went to her desk. She took up a quill pen, a clean parchment, wax. "My lord King?" She proffered the quill.

"It seems you planned this." Edward took the quill. "Was that the true reason for your smile, Eleanor? To mould me to your will with sweet manners and other blandishments?"

"You wound me, my gracious lord." She cast down her gaze, eyes shaded by her long lashes. *What have I become*? she thought. *A bold liar!* "I ask only for the sake of Lord Ralph."

"Ralph shall have his peace—and my venison, then," muttered Edward. "I trust you will reward me, Eleanor, for my kindness?"

"As ever, my lord husband," she said, watching over his shoulder as he wrote out the words that freed Lord Sudeley from his parliamentary duties. "After all, am I not your Queen—your secret Queen?"

CHAPTER TEN

More time passed in Great Dorset, the Wheel of the Year turning. In London, King Edward remained silent. Rents from the Wiltshire lands trickled in for Eleanor, but it seemed now she was not just Edward's secret queen but his forgotten one.

Eleanor had much time for reflection upon her life. She decided it was time to become a patron of Corpus Christi College in Cambridge. This patronage was something of a family tradition—her uncle, Henry Beauchamp, had endowed the college in the past. She had also promised Ralph Sudeley that she would do so, and have the College pray in perpetuity for the souls of Thomas and the Boteler family. With a tiny entourage of servants, she set off for the east with plans to visit Elizabeth after she was done in Cambridge.

The college town appeared wondrous to her eyes as she approached its gates on horseback. Airy spires and finials rose into a robin's egg blue sky. Stonework glowed like gold in the sunlight. Riding in past the green dome of Castle Hill, she crossed over the Great Bridge and past St Clements, the Round Church fashioned after the Holy Sepulchre in Jerusalem, and near to it, the House of the Franciscans. Then Barnwell Gate rose, turreted and manned, its portcullis a row of jagged teeth.

Waved past by the bored-looking guards, she wove her way through a tangle of streets full of scholars, monks, nuns, beggars and townsfolk until, beyond the high walls of the Augustinian priory, she spied the stone façade of Corpus Christi with the tower of St Ben'et's, the oldest church in all Cambridge, rising beside it like a stony finger, a grey shadow beside the warm Barnack stone of the College gateway.

Once inside College grounds, Eleanor's horse was taken for stabling and her servants guided to the hall for a meagre meal—Corpus Christi was one of the poorer colleges in Cambridge and could offer only bread and cheese. Eleanor herself was guided by one of the fellows to the office of the Master, Dr John Botwright, a spry, lean, white-haired man in his sixties whose hawk-like nose was topped by a tiny pair of imported Florentine spectacles with a polished bone frame.

"Lady Eleanor, sit…sit!" He gestured her to a bench which had been draped with a fine cloth covering just for her arrival. She glanced at the cloth, a gift to the college from a benefactor, with some bemusement, stitched as it was with the image of a hairy woodwose, a Wildman of the forest, and his equally hirsute wife.

"I am so pleased, Lady Eleanor, to make this acquaintance today," said Dr Botwright. "Your sister, the esteemed Duchess of Norfolk, has also been most generous to Corpus Christi."

"Although I cannot match my sister's gifts, for I am but a poor widow," said Eleanor, "I will do my very best for Corpus Christi, to the greater good of the scholars and to the glory of God."

The Master bowed his head. "Your largesse is much appreciated. You have probably heard that our College is, well, rather impoverished. We have lost much of our wealth over the years, alas. In the Peasant's Revolt, nigh on eighty years ago, a mob led by the mayor of Cambridge raided Corpus Christi and carried off all our plate. We had scarcely got back on our feet, relying on donations, when another riot took place but two years ago, and our income was spent on arrows, weapons and harness to protect what few goods we had acquired since the Revolt. A house of learning turned to a house of war; I tell you, madam, I had not thought to see such evil times in my tenure."

He shifted across his desk, fiddling with his spectacles; the magnifying glass made his eyes look huge, comical— Eleanor fought the urge to laugh, which would no doubt offend the old man, who was known to be highly efficient and somewhat dictatorial in manner.

"With help from God in heaven, may we flourish from now onwards," he said. "I can only pray that this new King brings good and not evil; I know him not, but hear he lives licentiously surrounded by his equally debauched fellows. Yet God, in his mysteries, granted him the victory."

Eleanor went hot then cold to hear Doctor Botwright speak so disparagingly of Edward. Then she remembered that Botwright had once been chaplain to King Henry himself and no doubt firmly espoused the Lancastrian cause.

Botwright must have seen her expression change and cleared his throat. "I will not say more; a fine Lady need not hear tales of the sordidness that occurs in the halls of the mighty far from our seat of learning!"

She bowed her head, eager to change the subject. Doctor Botwright cleared his throat. "I am an old man now, my Lady, and I have fallen behind in my daily work. I will leave you now in the care of one of the Fellows—I am thinking you might enjoy the company of Thomas Cosyn. Any paperwork that is necessary concerning your patronage shall be dealt with on the morrow when my schedule is clearer."

"Yes, of course, I understand that you are a busy man. I look forward to seeing Thomas Cosyn. As you must know, my sister and I have long been his personal patrons and were the ones to put forth his name as a Fellow. His family was well-known to our own esteemed Beauchamp forefathers; the Cosyns have had long had ties with the church on their estates."

Botwright gathered his dark robes and walked out into the courtyard, blinking in the bright sunlight like a wise, ancient owl. Beside a wall covered in sprays of growing purple flowers, leaned a young man of similar age to Eleanor, his nose buried in a large, leather-bound book.

"Thomas!" barked Dr Botwright. "You are needed. And what are you doing with that book out of the library where it could be rained on or thieved by some passer-by?"

The young man, Thomas Cosyn, slammed the book shut, sending a small dust cloud into the air. "Forgive me,

Master, but I was so intrigued, I could not put the book down…so I borrowed it."

"Against the rules!" Doctor Botwright waggled a finger as if the younger scholar was but a noughty schoolboy. "Hand it over and I shall return it to the library where it belongs. What was it anyway?"

"Aristotle." Cosyn passed the precious tome to the master. "One of the books left to us by the great Thomas Markaunt. I would have taken care with it, I swear, Master."

"I'm sure you intended to, Cosyn, but you know as well as I do that Proctor Markaunt donated over seventy books to Corpus Christi and already many have gone 'astray'. We cannot risk any more accidents…."

"No, of course, sir. I beg forgiveness, Master."

John Botwright thrust the tome under his arm and turned to Eleanor. "I trust you are happy to spend the rest of the afternoon in Cosyn's company, my Lady?"

"I am sure I will be fine, Master." Eleanor smiled over at Cosyn, who blushed to the roots of his close-cropped brown hair. "I would be most interested in hearing about the College from his perspective."

Botwright stalked off, long legs jerking beneath his midnight robes, the precious ancient book tucked safely under his arm. "Well," said Eleanor, facing Thomas Cosyns, "shall Eleanor faced Thomas Cousyn with a smile, "shall we begin, Master Cosyn?"

He cleared his throat. "As you wish, my Lady. I hope you will agree by the end of the day that your patronage of this great foundation—and my own humble person—is indeed a worthy cause!"

With Cosyns walking briskly before Eleanor, he showed her around the Old Court. "It is a little ruinous," he said ruefully, gesturing to the worn stonework, "and more than a little old-fashioned, with but a hall, pantry and buttery. There are two floors, and twenty-two rooms for Fellows and scholars. That said, there are but twelve of us. Plenty of room and spaces for contemplative study—but damned cold, pardon my language, Lady, in the dead of winter! We have to huddle around a fire in the hall, whether we want to see each other's faces that day or not."

"Such discomfort must come to an end," said Eleanor. "It is not conducive to study. Braziers must be obtained and if the money will extend, fireplaces and chimneys put in. Well, at least *one* fireplace to give you some cheer!"

She glanced around the Court, suddenly frowning. "Where do the Fellows worship? I see no chapel."

Cosyn gave a heavy sigh. "At Saint Ben'et's next door, Lady Eleanor. We have to leave the college premises and walk in the street to go to prayer."

She bit her lip, contemplative. "How unfitting—and concerning. Most colleges have their own chapels. One should be built, I deem, and until it is completed a walkway leading to St Ben'et's should be built on the inside of Corpus Christi. At least you will no longer have to leave the college precincts for prayer."

He led her onwards through the hall with its simple long trestle table and burnt out fire in a central pit. The walls were hazy with old ash and smoke, the glazed windows holding a yellow tint for the same reasons. "What do you dine on?" asked Eleanor. "Do you get enough supplies?"

"Other than the Feast of Corpus Christi, when we hold a sumptuous banquet...no!" He laughed a little nervously, glancing around as if he feared Master Botwright might be in the vicinity, listening. "Mutton and more mutton, I'm afraid. Maybe the odd pigeon-pie if we're lucky. And stockfish for Lent, of course—Jesu, how I've grown to dislike stockfish! You'll find, Lady Eleanor, that there aren't any fat Fellows at Corpus Christi."

"Another thing that needs to change. A man cannot study, whether it be the Word of God or philosophy, if he is hungry. I will see your food supplies are upped and will speak to the Duchess of Norfolk about the same."

"And wine? We seldom have wine save at the yearly banquet. All we are stuck with is small beer."

She gave him a look with raised eyebrows. "I'll see about wine—but it's not to misuse, do you understand, Thomas?"

Cosyn gave a short, joyous laugh, and for the first time in a long while, Eleanor felt her own mirth rise. A dark cloud lifted from her heart, now that she was far away from Great Dorset and her bittersweet memories of Edward. She felt useful as she had not done in the past; her endowment would do good for others, not least of all the souls of her dead first husband and his kin. She mattered and was not just a cast-off wife caught in an entanglement she could speak of to none, not even her confessor.

"I have dwelt on the bad points of Corpus Christi, my Lady," Cosyn continued, "but now you must see our treasures—few but fulsome."

He led her upstairs into the library, a small chamber nestled against the Master's Lodge. Inside, the close air smelt of parchment, vellum, leather and dust. The librarian, a diminutive man with a balding pate and black hair springing from ears and brows, gave Thomas an admonishing look, grabbed a stack of books from a bench and began noisily filing them away. "Chain, we need chains," he murmured. "Too many people borrowing…without letting me know!"

"Don't pay attention to Thurstan, my Lady," said Cosyn with a gallant air. "He always has the temperament of a kicked cat."

The librarian spluttered, seeming to notice Eleanor for the first time. Short-sighted, he squinted at her. "My Lady, forgive my manners. Now I must get to work!" Red-faced, he shuffled off with books bulging under his spindly arms.

Grinning, Thomas Cosyn led Eleanor into yet another room through an iron-bound door he unlocked with a key attached to his belt. "Inside lie the treasures of Corpus Christi," he said mysteriously, eyes sparkling.

Inside the room stood a huge broad chest carved from oak. Thomas raised the lid and pointed to some objects within. "These were gifts that survived the rioting of King

Richard's reign last century. The mighty drinking horn, made from the horn of a beast that no longer treads this mortal earth, is as old as creation itself. And the Swan Mazer, is…is something of a jest."

"How so?" Eleanor peered into the chest. A mazer was a little drinking bowl used at feasts and celebrations.

Thomas bent and reverently lifted the mazer in both hands. A swan with outspread wings and gaping beak rose on a column from a central boss. "If you drink too deeply and the mazer is overfull, the wine will run down the column, which is a syphon, and drench the drinker! Not that we have much wine here as I told you! The bowl is a magic thing of great craftsmanship, is it not? It has a spell on it too, here, beneath the cover with its silvered strawberry leaves— *Jasper, Balthasar, Melchoir…*"

Eleanor crossed herself for safety at hearing the incantation.

Thomas Cosyn hastily put the mazer away and closed the chest lid. "My Lady, I did not mean to startle you. Believe me, we have no baneful necromancers dwelling in our hallowed halls!"

The tour of the College over, Thomas led Eleanor back into the Old Court where the sun was reddening the stonework as it descended into the west.

Eleanor glanced at the waning light with alarm. "I had not thought the hour so late! My servants must be summoned so that we can travel onwards to my lodgings. Can you get them for me, dear Cosyn? And tell Master Botwright that I shall arrive before Nones tomorrow to sign the necessary documents for the endowment."

"I will see that all is done, Lady Eleanor," said Cosyn "and I thank you again for your graciousness in your patronage. Who knows how high I may rise one day because of your kindness? When Master Botwright retires—long may it be before he does—who knows? And if I ever ascend to his exalted position, not only will I do all the work here you've spoken of, I will have a little Talbot hound carved in stone and placed upon the gable in memory of the generosity of the Talbot family."

"I look forward to seeing it someday," said Eleanor with a smile, and she felt again the warm rush in her heart that she had experienced earlier. A strange contentment, happiness through loss and grief.

Time would heal her wounds. More or less.

CHAPTER ELEVEN

"I wish to stay in the east, Bet." Eleanor sat in the solar of Framlingham Castle with her sister Elizabeth, Duchess of Norfolk. "I do not desire to return to Warwickshire."

Elizabeth eyed her quizzically. "I will help you, if that is your desire, Nel, but I am surprised. You seemed happy there last we met."

"Much has changed." Eleanor toyed with the rings on her fingers. "I…I do not know if I wish to see Great Dorset again. My steward will maintain the manor for me. I have Agnes coming from Dorset with my poor dear old Blanchette—that's all I need from my old life."

"If it is truly in your heart to stay here, I would be most glad of it but I must speak to my husband John, and as you know, he is not quite of age yet and must parlay with his advisers."

"I would not burden you, Elizabeth; I don't wish to live at Framlingham, as fair to the eye as it is. I want to live more quietly, away from the workings of great men…" A shadow crossed her features.

"I have a house at East Hall," said Elizabeth, thoughtful. "The King confirmed it as part of my jointure."

Eleanor flinched at the mention of Edward.

Elizabeth instantly her discomfort. "Nel, it…it's about King Edward, isn't it? Why you want to leave Dorset and live near me, although not around the 'great men' who serve the King. His words to me, the message he gave…You were his mistress, weren't you? Oh, Nel, be not ashamed. You were lonely and still youthful; he is handsome and lusty, and, I dare say, persistent in seeking his pleasures. Most women would have done the same; it is hard to refuse a King. Neither you nor he committed more than the sin of fornication, which can be forgiven! You are not adulterers."

Eleanor grew pale; she fiddled with the end of her veil, dragging it across her face as if to hide her shame. "It…it is more complicated than that, Elizabeth. I still cannot say the truth of what went between us. I do not worry so much for my immortal soul, I will seek penance for my sins…but it is Edward I fear for."

"I wouldn't, Nel." Elizabeth's voice was quiet but firm. "He will have many sins to atone for due to his carnal ways, I'd wager. Eleanor, if you do not already know, he has a bastard son born just this year. He has named him Arthur after the great king of old."

Eleanor's eyes widened; it was if she had been struck a blow, despite her desire to leave her old life behind. "A son! Who is his mother?"

"A wanton wench called Elizabeth Wayte, 'tis said. Or rather, Elizabeth Lucy now—Edward married her off to a member of the Calais garrison to give her some respectability. He still beds her, though, when he can, or so I've heard. Oh, Nel, do not weep, I cannot bear it…"

Eleanor wiped at her eyes. "He mentioned the Wayte family to me in Wiltshire, where he gave me lands. Little did I know his true connection with them. While he was buying me off with property, he was swiving the Wayte girl behind my back."

Elizabeth was stunned into silence. She had never heard her pious, quiet-voiced sister used such harsh and unladylike language, even in anger.

Nervous and agitated, Eleanor rose from her stool. "I should not have spoken thus in front of you. Forgive me, my sister. I am merely shocked, though why I should be, I know not. It should be no surprise he was untrue."

"You must marry again," said Elizabeth with determination. "You must put the King from your mind and find another who will make you his lawful wife. John and I will help you"

"No…*NO!*" Eleanor raced to the window, bracing herself in the frame as if contemplating hurling herself out into the courtyard below. Elizabeth gasped, her hand pressed to her mouth in horror. Had her beloved older sister lost her mind?

Then Eleanor turned back towards her, gasping and trembling, her hands clenching and unclenching at her sides. "I had sworn to never say ought to you but now I feel I must. Elizabeth, Edward is my lawful husband. We married in secret in Dorset."

Shocked, he young Duchess jumped up, and then sat down again in a flurry, her own legs going out from under her. Eleanor rushed from the window and the two sisters embraced, Eleanor weeping against the blue velvet of Elizabeth's gown.

"Married!" whispered Elizabeth. "Are you certain? Oh, forgive me, what a stupid thing to say!"

Eleanor nodded weakly. "It was done properly. Not just words. He bought a Canon with him—Canon Stillington."

"Stillington…Lord Privy Seal. Men whisper that he is under consideration for a future Bishopric. Who else was there?"

"Edward's friend, Lord Hastings; he will say nothing."

"No, that he will not. He is Edward's partner in vice, despite the difference in their ages."

Elizabeth disentangled herself from her sister's embrace and began to pace the room. "A great dishonour has been done to our family. I must confer with John…"

"I beg you, Elizabeth, if you love me, tell no one." Eleanor groped at the cuff of Elizabeth's sleeve in desperation. "I fear what would happen if the truth got out. You would be at odds with the King…it must never happen. We must stay silent for our own safety."

"Surely, you do not think…"

"I do not know. All I know is that I do not wish to risk it. To risk you. If he has repudiated me, and it seems he has, let that be an end to the matter."

"But you can never marry again, such a marriage would be bigamous."

"I have no intention of marrying. Over these past weeks, my mind has found some ease thinking of other things. Our endowment of Corpus Christi, my faith in the Lord Jesus Christ and his Mother. I...I have decided to join a religious order, the Carmelites. I hear they have a goodly house in Norwich. I won't become a nun, but I shall join the order as a tertiary and dedicate the rest of my day to good works to atone for my sinful folly."

Norwich's walls, heavily towered, rose on the horizon, dwarfed by the cathedral of the Holy Trinity, built by master masons with golden stone imported from Caen. Sadly, the spire, once the second tallest in the land, was truncated, sticking out of the surrounding houses like a craggy black tooth—lightning had struck it earlier in the year, sending flames running down the timber supports and through the cathedral nave, causing terrible damage.

"Are you sure about this, my Lady?" Mounted on a placid pony, Agnes trotted along at Eleanor's side. She was newly arrived from Great Dorset to serve her mistress in her new residence—the Duchess Elizabeth's fine manor of East Hall—and was warily peering about her at the unfamiliar town.

"I have never been surer of anything, Agnes," said Eleanor, and the maid could not deny her mistress looked bright-eyed and joyous, not the moping troubled creature who had waited for news that never came to Dorset.

The little entourage, the two women, plus their mounts and a company of guards, approached Bishopgate, crossing Bishop's Bridge over the churning waters of the River Wensum. In the centre of the bridge a strong tower faced them, its arrow-slits like narrowed, hostile eyes, its round door an open maw. The watchtower was manned by the local monks, who had permission to take tolls from passers-by— one of them, waddling like a duck, his cassock straining over his belly, came hurrying towards them with his hand outstretched.

"You rude man, you could have asked and not stood there with your hand out like a beggar," Agnes admonished, but Eleanor just smiled sweetly at the sweating friar and dropped coins into his palm one by one.

Passing over the last arch of the bridge with its ramshackle houses, the companions travelled up the street past the Great Hospital where thirteen pauper clergymen were cared for. A queen had visited the church there once, long ago—Anne of Bohemia, wife of the ill-starred Richard II. Her heraldic eagles still flew, dark-winged, across the decorated ceiling. For all that had happened in her husband's fateful reign, she was loved and she was remembered—the irony of it was not lost on Eleanor Talbot as she rode by.

Soon she could once again smell the foetid scent of the river Wensum. Glancing to one side, she noticed the bulk of Cow Tower, one of the great defences of Norwich, and knew she was near her destination at Whitefriars. Clucking to her mare, she urged the beast to greater speed. She wanted this journey to be over with. For one chapter of her life to close and another to begin. A rebirth, from sin to purity, with the aid of the Blessed Virgin, to whom she had ever been devoted.

The little company turned a corner, pushing through throngs of urchins, merchants and monks in all colours of habits, grey, white, black and brown. A parish church, St James Pockthorpe, stood at the end of the road, its flint tower and slate roof shining in the wan sunlight. Beyond it, with lands stretching towards the Wensum, stood a large, rich-looking monastic house behind a low wall.

At last! Whitefriars, home of the Norwich Carmelites.

Heart beginning to pound, Eleanor proceeded toward the entrance. Before her rose a mighty portal arch, richly carved with figures—the Virgin Mary and St Anne, the stern-faced prince Edmund Crouchback, son of Henry III, all rising in splendour amidst a wild, almost pagan, tangle of leaves, grapes and vines.

Taking a deep breath, she dismounted her horse and, giving the reins to an attendant, stepped under the candlelit arch, inhaling the smoky, incense-heavy air.

The prior's chamber was warm and bright, lit by a small fire in an iron brazier. The walls were painted with scenes from the Virgin's life, the Well of Elijah on Mount Carmel and a portrait of the order's founder, Berthold of Calabria, dressed in the armour of a Crusader. Above Berthold, on scrollwork along the edge of the ceiling was engraved the Carmelite motto: *Ordo Fratrum Beatissimæ Virginis Mariæ de Monte Carmelo.*

Prior Richard Walter, a well-built man just past middle-age, peered at Eleanor over his desk; he held an open letter in his hand. "I have here a missive from Sir John Howard, sent on your behalf, regarding your initiation as a tertiary of the Carmelite order. Is that correct, Lady Eleanor?"

"It is correct, Prior Walter. John Howard is kin to my sister's husband and kindly offered to vouch for me."

So..." The prior's keen brown eyes scanned the contents of the letter. "You wish to join the Carmelites as a layperson, rather than becoming a nun with a different order—as the Carmel has no nuns here in England as yet."

"Yes, that is my wish. I desire to serve and to devote myself to God rather than the profane world, but I have been worldly too long to be wholly cloistered in a convent."

Nodding, the prior read onwards. "Have you a residence within reach of the Carmel House? If you are to be made a tertiary, you need an unchanging abode."

"Yes, prior, I do. The Duchess Elizabeth, my sister, has kindly offered me the use of her house, End Hall, at Kenninghall."

The old man's face, which until now had been stern and austere, lightened. "Ah, Kenninghall! I know it well. The famed John Kenyngale, once prior here at Whitefriars, haled from Kenninghall. He was the Father Provincial of our order and built our library. He was also the personal chaplain of Richard of York, the late father of our King, Edward IV."

Eleanor jolted upright at the unexpected naming of her secret husband. She prayed her face had not given away too many of her emotions.

Prior Richard was eyeing her over the top of John Howard's letter. "You seem dismayed. Is something not to your liking, Lady Eleanor?"

"No, no, everything is fine. I am just a little weary from the road." She drew her cloak more tightly about her.

"If all is to your satisfaction, then I will show you this House of God." The Prior got to his feet, reaching for a cane which he used to support himself. Leaving the chamber by three worn stone steps, he escorted Eleanor through the cloister, its pillars carved with rich foliage like the external portal, but also draped in real vines heavy with fragrant flowers.

As he walked, his cane tapping the bright floor-tiles with their decorative lions and shields, he pointed out features—carvings of the Magdalen, a large stone image of St Anne painted in bright colours. "We plan to put in a chapel to blessed Thomas a Becket," said the Prior, "but funds being what they are, it may not happen for some years yet. There is also an attached chamber for an anchorite or anchoress to dwell in."

"And is there one present now?" asked Eleanor. She knew Norwich was famous for its female religious mystics such as Julian or Marjory Kempe, who locked themselves within four small walls to transcend impure flesh and be closer to God through the strength of their minds.

"No." The prior shook his head. "The last was Lady Emma Stapleton, daughter of Sir Miles, who dwelt enclosed for over twenty years. Prior Hemlyngton, a noted scholar and theologian was her spiritual advisor. Mayhap one will come again—this is a town well acquainted with holy women."

Escorting Eleanor into the friary church, he pointed down the long nave with its graceful pillars and fan-vaulted roof. Painted glass sent colours dancing across the clean tiles. "It is one of the largest churches in Norwich," he said. "God has been good to us, and Our Lady of Mount Carmel, to whom we are dedicated."

He turned to face the young woman. "Our main *charism* is contemplation of the divine brought about through prayer and service. You, my Lady, upon becoming a tertiary, must immerse yourself in liturgical prayer even as we at Whitefriars. It would do well for you to follow our rules— that meat shall be eaten no more than three days a week, and that fasting should take place from Holy Cross Day until Easter."

"I shall obey as best I am able, I swear to you, Prior." Eleanor bowed her head. "I have read the holy book *The Cloud of Unknowing*, and taken its words to heart—'look forward, not backwards.'"

Prior Walter seemed impressed by her statement, a small smile playing on his thin lips. "Those words are wise, and there are more, I remember, from the same manuscript: *God is a jealous lover, and brooks no rival.*"

Eleanor flushed, wondering if the Prior had heard some rumour, but she doubted anything had reached so far East. In all likelihood, he merely warned her against entanglements of the heart that would take her from the path of righteousness— although a tertiary, unlike a nun, was permitted to be married.

"Who could rival God?" she murmured, but she would not meet the Prior's eyes, pretending to cast her gaze modestly down upon the tiles.

Who, indeed?

CHAPTER TWELVE

"I don't want to do this, mother!" Elizabeth Woodville glared at Jacquetta of Luxembourg, as the older woman pinched her cheeks to make them rosy and applied crushed cherries to her lips. "I feel an utter fool!" Outside the chamber door, a gaggle of younger girls, angelically fair, long blond locks hanging loose to their waists, were giggling and elbowing each other. Elizabeth's numerous sisters.

"You will not feel such a fool if you get what you want," said Jacquetta sternly. She was a tall, stately woman with a generous mouth and dark amber hair encased in a rather old-fashioned netted headdress. "Listen to me, my girl, and the world will fall at your feet."

"I do not want the world," Elizabeth sighed. "All I want is my sons' inheritance restored and some money to live on. I am near destitute."

"You know you are welcome at Grafton, Bess," said Jacquetta. "You can stay until you find another husband, and as you are known to the court as a great beauty, that should not take long if you are wise in your decisions."

"I have nothing of value save my looks; it may not be as easy as you think. If only my father *were*…"

Jacquetta cast her eldest daughter a warning frown. At seventeen she had married John of Lancaster, Duke of Bedford, the brother of Henry V—a marriage of high repute and great success, despite the age difference between young Jacquetta and her much older husband. However, after John died at his castle of Joyeus Repos near Rouen, she had swiftly fallen in love with a dashing young knight called Richard Woodville who was tasked with escorting her to England—and married him in a secret ceremony. The scandal caused quite a stir and King Henry VI fined the couple £1000 for wedding without a licence. The marriage had proved fruitful, with fourteen children born in quick succession, yet many courtiers still scorned Jacquetta for marrying below her station. However, she would not brook any insolence from her own children.

Elizabeth noticed her mother's expression and glanced aside, her gaze coming to rest on her gawking sisters peering through the doorway. They let out shrieks of laughter as she grasped an ornamental comb from a tray of toiletries and hurled it with all her force at the girls.

Their mirth became feigned squeals of terror as they scattered like skittles in a schoolboy's game, their feet pattering on the creaking floorboards of the manor house as they ran.

"They need a good birching, mother!" Elizabeth glowered.

"No more than you do, daughter," said Jacquetta, mouth pursed in frustration. "Now get that ugly glower off your face, child. He won't want to see you scowling and scrunched-up like some church grotesque."

Elizabeth continued to pout, her lower lip outthrust like that of a petulant child. A *pretty* petulant child, however, with a full, red lower lip and sleepy, sensual eyes as green as the grass in spring.

Jacquetta was glad when her moody widowed daughter finally began to study her face in a small hand-glass given her upon her wedding day to John Grey of Groby, now lying in a cold grave after being struck down at the second battle of St Alban's. Studying and looking rather pleased with what she saw.

Jacquetta smiled a secret little smile and fingered the small clay figurines in the pouch attached to her girdle. A man, a woman, crudely wrought. Around them was bound a strip of parchment written upon in moon-blood.

'*Edwardus Rex*' it said.

The King galloped through the woodland of the Old Park outside the village of Grafton. A fine day for hunting, before settling down to business, but there was one major problem—no one had spotted a single stag all day. The huntsmen were walking dispiritedly about in the greenwood, seeking animal spore; the lymer hounds were milling in confusion through the ferns, unable to pick up a scent.

"Well, I certainly hope the rest of the day proves more entertaining than this," Edward said to Will Hastings, who was riding at his side. "I can't imagine it will be, though—listening to the pleas of some Lancastrian widow-woman who has lost her dower lands in some family dispute."

"Oh, I think you may find this meeting more interesting than you think." Will winked at his friend.

"Truly? In what way?" Edward looked doubtful.

"It's Elizabeth Grey...*Woodville*," said Hastings. "Don't you remember, Ned? At court. A long time ago, admittedly."

Edward frowned and shook his head. "The name is familiar. I think my father once wrote a letter to her, commending a knight called Sir Hugh Johns. Johns was enamoured to distraction but she turned down a proposal of marriage and married another. I cannot say I recall this Woodville wench myself...but I wasn't at court much, in the old days. My father feared the danger and kept me and Edmund at Ludlow. I've been to Grafton before, though, just after I became King—I saw lots of tow-headed Woodville maids, but most were not much higher than my knee!"

"I expect when you became King, she was still at Astley Manor, wrangling over her dower lands with old Lady Ferrers, her mother-in-law," laughed Hastings. "In any case, Elizabeth is exceptionally beautiful, some say the greatest beauty in England."

"And you didn't go after her yourself?" Edward raised a quizzical eyebrow.

"Ah, I fear I would not be deemed good enough, Ned."

"Not good enough? Richard Woodville, her father, is but a commoner."

"But there is the mother to deal with, Jacquetta of Luxembourg. Royal-blooded in her own country and even descended long ago from several English Kings. A headstrong lass herself once—and some say a witch."

"A witch," Edward repeated, voice dripping scorn. "Really, Will. Witches."

"She was frequently overheard talking about her family's descent from the water-spirit, Melusine."

Edward made a dismissive noise. "The Plantagenets also claim such descent, and so they were called 'The Devil's Brood.' Well, if Jacquetta and her daughter are witches, then I am the Devil's own descendant, so I will conquer their baneful sorcery with my own!"

"You might *like* to be enchanted." Hastings grinned again. "Who knows?"

"Who knows indeed?" said Edward, and with that, he gave his steed its head and struck his spurs to its flanks, and he flew through the light-and-dark dappled forest, leaving Hastings and the huntsmen and hounds far behind.

On his swift steed, the young King soon covered much ground. Edward could hear the huntsmen's horns in the distance and imagined the chaos when they realised the King had well and truly disappeared. He smiled with playful malice. It was good to have a little time free of the fawning and the faithful alike. Even Hastings could grow tiresome every now and then. Here he could enjoy himself with a leisurely gallop before he had to submit to the tedium of Widow Grey's complaints. Beautiful—he doubted it. Probably grown as round as an old sow and as bristly as one too....

The forest began to clear, oaks and birches thinning out and allowing in a stream of pallid sunlight. Spores blew up beneath the horse's hooves, shining like faerie dust in the wavering light. An odd quietness seemed to fall over the woodland; the birds, the animals, even the wind grew suddenly, ominously still.

Despite himself, Edward felt a small shiver run the length of his spine. Had he taken Will's blathering about witches and enchantment too seriously? He hauled on the reins, bringing his horse down from a gallop to a brisk trot.

"Stand still, Thomas, or I will birch you!" A woman's voice drifted to his ears through the tangles of foliage. Not quite an enchantress' blandishments, but the young voice, mingled between nervousness and imperiousness, sounded intriguing nonetheless.

He edged his horse towards the voice. Passing through a thorny hedge, he saw the path open up and become wide, rutted with cart tracks. Several huge old oaks, bark gnarled into almost-demonic faces, flanked the edge of the path, and below the largest tree stood a woman holding two little boys by the hand.

His breath caught in his throat. It was as if he had indeed been ensorceled in that fatal moment. She was…*magnificent.* If she were a witch, he'd gladly succumb to her spell—for a while, at any rate. Tall and graceful, she held herself with the elegance of a queen, even as she tugged at the hand of the elder boy, who was throwing some sort of childish tantrum. Light welled through her milk-white skin, glimmered on her brow where, at the front of a modest henin, he caught the gleam of silver-gilt hair. Red lips parted enticingly as she sought to admonish the errant child again, while the lad whined in a petulant fashion and stomped his foot.

"I want to go, mother! It's cold out here in this beastly wood! I want to play with the other boys in Grafton!"

"Thomas, I told you…" She raised a slender hand, lily-pale, as if ready to smack the insolent child.

And then she saw Edward on his horse, cheeks flushed from the speed at which he'd ridden, his dark blue velvet cloak and cap glowing like jewels, his long legs clad in tight leather boots affixed with spurs of gold.

She knew at once who she faced in the woods; indeed, she had been waiting for him, having sent an old loyal servant of her mother's foraging along the road in order to bring back news of the King's party. But she had not expected him to reach Grafton quite so soon, nor had she expected him to arrive on his own, and she certainly had not expected him at the exact moment she was chastising her unruly son, Thomas.

"Your Grace," she breathed, her voice tremulous, and she sank gracefully to her knees, grasping her small sons' hands and pulling them down beside her. Thomas was silent now, round-eyed; the younger boy, Richard, cowered down behind his mother as much as he was able.

"Rise, rise," Edward said impatiently, drinking in the sight of her, the purity of her brow, the white swan's neck, the tempting marble flesh at the neck of her brocade gown... And, oh Jesu, when she looked up at him with those sleepy, secret and languorous eyes, half-shaded by curling dark-gold lashes—

He had to have her.

At any price.

"Your name, madame," he inquired although he already knew. It was Dame Grey, formerly Woodville, the widow come to plead for her lands. Right now, he was minded to hand them to her on a silver platter, but he could not do that, naturally; procedures must be followed. But he certainly would listen to *anything* she might say...

"I am Elizabeth..." she hesitated, "Woodville."

Edward smiled down at her, all charm, eager to impress this cool beauty. "And the little warriors with you are?"

"My eldest son, Thomas Grey, and my younger, Richard."

"Are you really the King?" asked Thomas boldly, eyeing the huge man on the horse. "Where's your crown?"

"Thomas!" Elizabeth snapped, irritated once again by her boy's wilful behaviour.

"I don't wear a crown all the time, young Thomas," laughed Edward, swinging out of his saddle and taking hold of the reins of his horse. "It gets rather heavy when one is performing *other* activities." His gaze travelled from Thomas's round pink-and-white face to his mother's lovely visage—and lingered.

"You are as tall as a giant!" Young Richard Grey, just five years old, stared up in wonder at the King from beneath a thatch of white-blond curls.

"You can be a giant too!" laughed Edward, and to Elizabeth Woodville's obvious surprise, he whisked up her small son and set him atop his ornate saddle. "Now look at you—you're above your King!"

"Your Grace, I...I don't..." Elizabeth was at a loss for words.

"Don't fear, Lady. I won't let your son fall. Let us walk back to the manor at Grafton, and you may tell me of your woes upon the way. Lead on, Madam."

Dragging her long skirts off the mud on the path and with Thomas running wild before her, Elizabeth told Edward of her plight, how she had been made homeless and penniless by her husband's death and was forced to return to her family home.

"But Madame, what can you expect?" said Edward, trudging along the muddy path. "Your late husband was my enemy. Firmly Lancastrian, as are your family, unless their hearts have turned utterly."

"Oh, my lord King, they are nothing but loyal to you now!" cried Elizabeth. "You must believe me!"

"How could I not, Madam. Such a fair mouth as yours would never sully itself with a lie."

She blushed prettily. But she was clearly not going to let the subject go. "The problem is not about John's lands anyway, your Grace. If they are gone for the part he played in warfare, they are gone. It is my dower lands that are in question—those are rightfully mine, no matter what. John's mother, Baroness Ferrers will not hand them over. She hates me for some reason...."

"Who could hate such a gracious lady as you?" Edward smiled down at her, eyes twinkling.

"Well, she does, your Grace; I have no idea why. Even if the Baroness despises me, I deem it cruel that she leaves my boys, her own grandsons, with nothing."

"I shall consider your request of an intercession, Dame Grey, but I must look into the matter further. I cannot make the decision immediately and without hearing from Baroness Ferrers."

Elizabeth began to pout, but hastily hid her disappointment and put on a false smile. "My thanks, your Grace."

"Can I call you Elizabeth?" asked the King.

She coloured again. "Your Grace can call me whatever he desires!"

"Elizabeth it is then. And you...you may call me Edward in *private*, of course."

Again, the flash of hectic colour to her cheeks and, Edward thought, a deepening of the forest hue of her eyes. It enchanted him, sent a thrill of desire through him. Hunting deer? No, forget the hunt, he had found what he truly wanted to catch today...

"Edward," Elizabeth whispered, her lashes fluttering. "If it your wish, Edward it shall be, your Grace."

The King's company found lodgings for the night in the village of Grafton and beyond. Edward strolled through the streets, basking in the admiration of the cheering villagers before returning to Grafton Manor for a feast with the Woodville family.

Entering the small but neat hall of the Manor, decorated with the best quality imported Arras (Jacquetta had retained her continental tastes), he was greeted by the entire family, including the eldest son, Anthony, who had ridden in from his own lands to be in attendance. All the Woodvilles went down like a row of skittles, bowing and bobbing, a sea of handsome men and pretty fair-haired girls.

Edward smiled benevolently at his hosts and their family, walking around them in his great long-toed poulaines, his deep red velvet robe and his chain of gem-studded suns and roses. At length, he gestured for the womenfolk to rise; with a rustle of skirts and headdresses and flowing hair for the unwed girls, they all hurried to their allotted benches, leaving the menfolk kneeling.

Edward smirked down at Sir Richard Woodville and Anthony. Richard was a man past middle life but still trim and hale, his hair barely touched by a hint of silver. Anthony was slim, tall, urbane, well-dressed, resembling his sister Elizabeth in the cast of his face, although the shining cap of his hair was a rich brown instead of blonde.

"Oh, how lovely it is to see you two gentlemen again," said Edward. "No, I *do* mean it, fear not. It is time to put old enmities behind and move forward. Rise and be seated."

Looking somewhat startled, the two men clambered up and retreated hastily to their seats, their faces aflame. On her bench, Jacquetta was equally florid, while Elizabeth was stiff as a frozen statue. An incident had taken place in 1460 before Edward had become King. The Woodvilles, firm Lancastrians, had been in Sandwich involved in building a fleet of ships for Henry Beaufort. Following the orders of Warwick and Edward, Sir John Dynham had crept up on them in the night and captured Sir Richard, Jacquetta and Anthony in their beds. Jacquetta was freed from incarceration almost immediately, but the other two were taken before the Earl of Warwick, the Earl of March and old Salisbury, who berated them publicly before an assembly of lords. "You are a knave's son," Salisbury had sneered at Sir John. "You are but an esquire who made yourself through marriage," Warwick had added, following his father's lead, while Edward had laughed at the prisoners and loudly agreed with his kinsmen that they were foolish, puffed up nobodies, now soundly humiliated for all the world to see.

Yet here he was now, King of England, all friendliness and smiles, yet reminding them of that terrible, embarrassing day. The subtle threat—*do as I will or it will go ill for you*—was there, despite his smiles. And yet seemingly he offered them peace, and even more: a chance to flourish in his new regime?

Edward took his place under a hastily-erected canopy, and his own troupe of musicians entered the hall and began to play on lutes and harps. Dressed in her best, wearing amber silk and with her hair wrapped under a caul and gauzy veil, Jacquetta sidled over to Anthony and her husband. "Take these," she whispered, handing each of them a white rose newly plucked from the manor gardens. "Let him know where our loyalties now lie."

"Wife…" began Sir Richard, frowning.

"No, not a word of protest. You know well how the Wheel of Fate has turned. Well, turn again it might if this family is clever and careful. And I know we are all clever here."

"Mother, what do you mean?" Anthony looked earnestly at Jacquetta. "What are you planning?"

She gave a little nod in Elizabeth's direction; her daughter was having her hands laved in a silvered bowl, first amongst the Woodville sisters. "Elizabeth is our crown jewel, Anthony. *Crown* jewel…"

"Bess has always meant the world to me, and yes, there is no woman on earth like her, but I do not understand…"

"Anthony, usually you are more adept than this! Look how he gazes at her…the King! It is clear to any who have eyes to see that he finds her attractive."

Anthony sat back on his bench, shaking his head, his face full of worry. "Mother, do not encourage her in this matter. You don't know of the King's *appetites*. He takes, then discards. I would not see my sister misused in such a fashion."

"You won't," assured Jacquetta. "Elizabeth is no fool and no man's toy. Now, come, look happy. And make sure Edward sees you and your father with your roses!"

After the banquet, the King retired to the allotted rooms with his gentlemen. The Woodville women were all crowded into Jacquetta's chamber, the youngest children giggling on pallets on the floor, while Elizabeth and her sister Anne climbed into their mothers' bed with its counterpane stitched with gilded pineapples. As she went about the chamber snuffing the candles, Jacquetta called Elizabeth to come and speak to her a moment.

Pushing aside the coverlet, the young widow got up and walked towards her mother, her long, unbound hair a cascade of moonlight down to her hips. "What is it, Lady Mother? Could you not have spoken ere I readied myself for bed? My feet are cold." She hugged herself, dancing in discomfort on the freezing floor-tiles.

Jacquetta shook her head. "Stop complaining, Elizabeth. I need you alone."

Hastily she led her daughter behind a painted screen for privacy, which may have been unnecessary, since there was so much squealing from the younger girls as they tussled on their pallets there was no chance anyone would overhear a word that was spoken.

"What have I done, mother?" asked Elizabeth, folding her arms defensively over her kirtle, sure she was to be chided for some unknown gauche blunder at table.

"Nothing wrong—and may you keep it that way. The King is interested…he is interested in you."

Elizabeth sputtered. "No, he cannot be. Well, perhaps he was *looking* at me, and I at him, but he is the *KING*, mother, and he has a reputation. I, too, have a reputation, vastly different from Edward's—and I would not fain lose it."

"That is as it should be," smiled Jacquetta. "Listen, child, and listen well. You must hold the wolf at bay, yet hold out the promise of tender flesh."

"Ooh, mother…" Elizabeth made a disapproving face. "Whatever for, it's not as if he would marry me."

"We must make him *want* to marry you."

"Make him? How can one do such a thing? I am not a highborn princess, I am not a wealthy heiress. I am not even an untouched maiden; I have given birth to two babes…"

"Your allure may be stronger than you realise, Bess. Trust your mother. And there is always the mommets…" She reached to her belt pouch and brought out the two little clay poppets with the King's name woven around them.

"Mother!" Elizabeth's eyes widened. "Put that away! Get rid of it! If any were to find out…"

"No one will know, and you, my dearest, beautiful child—you will be queen. Just do as I tell you. Meet Edward in the gardens tomorrow, I will keep the girls—and Anthony—well away. Enchant the King, keep him keen, but do not give away what is most precious without recompense."

"Recompense?"

"A crown, my most lovely child. A crown."

The garden was filled with the scents of spring—rich, rain-soaked earth, the sweet buds of Primroses, the Marsh Marigolds sacred to the Virgin, the blue Forget-Me-Nots that were sacred to parted lovers.

Elizabeth sat on a little stone bench, jewel-like, pristine, her white veils floating about the marble beauty of her visage, her slender hands clasped in her lap. She wore green silk slashed with vivid red upon the sleeves and under-kirtle, the colours of life, of growing things…and of desire. The silk swished softly in a warm wind blowing from the south; its radiant hue made her eyes truly the hue of emeralds.

Edward towered above her, the victor of Towton—and the victor over many ladies' virtue. He was King; who would dare deny this smiling, beautiful but dangerous young man anything he desired? He leaned indolently on the stone canopy framing Elizabeth's seat, gazing down at her with a burning hunger.

"Bess," he said, "your dower lands...I have decided. They will all be returned to you and your boys, and damn old Lady Ferrers to hell. But I must ask you for something in return..."

"My Lord King?" Her thin, moon-pale brows lifted. "I have nothing. I am not wealthy."

"Oh, you have something indeed. Better than any money...With it, you can show me your great gratitude for retrieving your lands."

"Your Grace, I still know not what you mean. But I assure you, I will be grateful for your largesse all my natural life."

"Then show me your gratitude." He bent over her, his mouth claiming hers in a hard kiss, a kiss of possession more than that of a tender lover.

"Your Grace, this is not proper—my family is only a few feet away." She broke the kiss, shaking her head.

"Do they spy on your every move?"

"They have care for my honour...and so do I."

"Honour—pah. A woman's honour is overrated, madam. Jesu, I've never seen a woman I've desired more than you. Never..." He halted for a moment, eyes glazing over as if he suddenly remembered something, someone, from far away, another time.

Elizabeth saw that look and did not like it one bit. She had to play this game to its end, as her mother had advised her. Edward's attention must now be on her and no other. She must seem alluring yet innocent, yielding but in the end firm in defence of her virtue

"I am flattered by your attention, my lord King, and I would lie if I said I was not equally attracted to you, but I would never compromise my honour. Not for any man. Not even a King."

Edward's face grew thunderous. "Women like you all say the same thing, almost to the word! It is not as if I would maltreat you, woman, should you cleave to me and be my mistress…"

He suddenly lunged at her, catching her around the waist and dragging her roughly towards him. Her hair came loose, spilling out like moon-kissed silver. "You want me, I can see it in your eyes, Elizabeth!" Edward gasped. "Do not toy with me!"

She tried to pull away; she got one arm free, but Edward had a hard grip on the other. She went down in a haze of emerald skirts and the King flung himself atop her, pinning her down. "I am not a man to force a woman," he panted, "but you inflame me, Bess—and I see in your eyes, in the frenzy of your breathing, in your sweet, sweet trembling mouth that despite your cold words, you desire me too!"

Elizabeth strove to push him off, which was useless, for his strength was immense. She fumbled at her stocking, which brought a grunt of surprised pleasure from the King, who thought she was intending to disrobe. However, unexpectedly, a small, sharp knife appeared in her hand, blade flashing in the sunlight.

That stopped Edward. He whipped away from Elizabeth, rolling over the lawn, crushing the new flowers beneath his weight. "You *dare*…!" he shouted, eyes sparking fury.

"I mean no harm to you, never that!" Elizabeth cried, and she brought the knife-edge up to her throat, pressing it against the great life-vein that pulsed there. "But I tell you truly, Edward of York, I would sooner my life's blood spill upon the earth than surrender to the carnal embraces of a man who is not my husband."

"Your sons, what of your sons' futures?" Edward pounded the ground with his fist as if he were an enraged child. "Think of them when you act like an outraged virgin!"

"If their rightful inheritance can only be obtained by yielding to you in the manner of a harlot, then they must learn to be simple souls and live on only what they can earn," said Elizabeth, voice heavy with sorrow.

Edward sat in silence for a moment, gaze furious, chest heaving beneath its casing of fine cloth and sparkling gems. "Bess, put down the dagger. It is not necessary. I could not bear it if you harmed yourself."

Elizabeth threw the knife into the grass; Edward kicked it into a nearby hedge with his boot. "You have bewitched me." He put his head in his hands. "Hastings warned me your family had witch's blood."

"I swear to you, I haven't…"

"What do you want, Bess?" Edward's voice rose again, hoarse with frustration. "What do you want that I may lie with you? Jewels? I will have the best Italian jewellers cut emeralds and rubies for you. Lands for your boys—they shall be as rich as earls. Good husbands for your sisters—I will see your family rise to greatness. Name your price, woman. Name it!"

She arose, grass-stained and dishevelled but cat-like in litheness and grace. Tree blossoms torn from the white May-trees blew around her like snow, alighting in her unbound tresses. "I will accept only one thing, Edward. If you want me—you must make me your wife."

"Wife!" Edward's face turned crimson and he looked as if he would explode. Elizabeth tried not to cower. He did not touch her, however, but ripped up a handful of flowers and hurled them wildly around the garden. "You do not know what you ask! Is there no other way?"

She drew herself up, pure hauteur, queenly, an ice princess. "There is no other way, your Grace. It is all…or nothing."

A wide cold moon hung over Grafton Woodville. May 1 had come, and the peasant folk danced round Maypoles in the villages of Northamptonshire and leapt over great bonfires that burned long into the night. Laughing couples sprang over the flames and, heels singed, crept into the woodlands to make temporary 'greenwood weddings', some for but one night, others for a year and a day.

In the tangle of oaks in the Park, an owl hooted, its eerie cry echoing through the night. A thin mist rose from the ground, coiling around the edge of the village dew-pond, hanging over the manor house gardens. Swathed in a heavy cloak, Edward, King of England,crept like a fugitive through the gloom, riding accompanied by just one young page from his lodgings at Stony Stratford five miles away down Watling Street.

Quietly he dismounted outside the door of Grafton Manor, gesturing to the page boy to likewise climb down from his saddle and take both horses to the nearby barn. Then he stood beneath the door, where one torch burnt in a sconce, waiting, while white moths battered him with trembling wings.

After a few minutes, footsteps scurried on the flagstones inside the hall. The door creaked open and out stepped Jacquetta of Luxembourg, cloaked and hooded, shielding a small glass-framed lantern within a fold of her mantle. Next to her crept Elizabeth, also wearing a deep hood, the smell of jasmine scent drifting from her garments to make Edward's head spin.

They passed silent and lightless St Mary's church, stones blue-tinted in the smoky moonlight, and crossed the rutted straight line of Watling Street into the fields that stretched on the other side.

"We must follow the path alongside the wall, your Grace," whispered Jacquetta, pointing to a narrow trackway winding like a white ribbon over the field towards a stand of night-shrouded trees. "Over by Shaw Wood."

"Can we not light a torch, sir?" asked the little page, tripping in the darkness away from the feeble, half-furled glow of Jacquetta's lantern.

The older woman looked at the boy, then the King, and shook her head firmly.

"No torches, Jack," said Edward to the lad, tousling the boy's hair. "Just follow in my footsteps and all will be well."

"Mother and I know the way, it's not boggy or dangerous," said Elizabeth. "St Mary and St Michael's hermitage belonged to our family for generations; it is only in the last thirty years that it was conveyed to the Abbey of St James in Northampton."

The track wound on, and the little party entered the black line of trees. All light died, the moon was clawed under by tree-boughs; the hoot of the lonely owl grew louder as the scrubby trees of Shaw Wood blended into the grappling, moss-helmed oaks of Whittlebury Forest.

"There…" Jacquetta pointed into the darkness through the haze of branches. "A rushlight burns."

Sure enough, a pallid, wavering light, eerie as a corpse candle, shone between the swaying boughs of the little grove. Edward's eyes narrowed; he felt magic abroad on this pagan eve and suspected he had indeed been bound in a witch's spell. But he would have Elizabeth at any cost. By God, he would have her.

He'd said the same before…Jesu, even Hastings had looked alarmed when, at table in the Inn at Stony Stratford, Edward had whispered his plans for the evening. "Ned, this is a *surprise*…I hardly know what to say!"

"Congratulations?" Edward's voice had a hard edge as he stabbed a chunk of beef with a knife.

"Well, yes, but, well, you know. What about Eleanor Talbot…"

"Do not speak that name, Will! I beg you…No, I bloody well *command* you."

Will's hand had scraped through his thinning hair; the usual grin was absent. "I know you want the Woodville girl, but this may all unravel. Stillington was at Great Dorset, he officiated, he knows…"

"Stillington also knows how to keep silent. He'll be a bishop soon enough if he continued to please me…and keeps his mouth shut."

"Ned..." Will shuffled about, fingers white on the stem of his pewter goblet, "Warwick's been talking about a marriage alliance. A foreign princess. You need to marry sooner rather than later, Ned—you know that. A *proper* marriage..."

"Let Warwick talk all he wants...I'll marry a princess when I'm good and ready. Besides, you old fool, if it all goes badly tonight, who will ever know what went on here?"

Will bit his lip. "The girl's family for one. They are not like the kin of the...other one. Eleanor's sister the Duchess of Norfolk may or may not know what transpired at Great Dorset...but this lot, Ned! Your exploits won't remain secret for long. The whole family will all know by the morn, all go gossiping...."

"A risk I will take."

A risk...

The young King peered ahead at the beckoning finger of light and then let his gaze descend on Elizabeth Woodville, fleet as some forest sprite in her concealing cloak. Again, a wave of desire washed over him. Damn the consequences, this graceful creature would be his that very night!

The trees bowed out, revealing a small chapel in a clearing. Old and in poor repair, a cloister stretched out from the chapel towards a small ancient hospital. A torch burned outside the chapel's open door, but the hospital was empty, a wall slumped over, a hole gaping in the roof. Its original purpose as a safe place for poor, sick men had long ended; the surrounding lands were put under the plough by St James' Abbey instead.

The party entered the chapel. An aged priest, almost monkey-like in his stance and wizened face, stood in his vestments. He blinked dully at the newcomers. "This is most irregular, my Lady..." He blinked at Jacquetta Woodville with red-rimmed and crusty eyes. The flames of candles in sconces flickered off their surfaces; the old man was half-blind with cataracts. Hands like crows' claws clutched his Bible.

"This may make it more palatable to you," said Jacquetta, thrusting a bag of coins in his direction. The old priest made a garbled noise and nearly dropped his Bible. Jacquetta put the money back into her belt-pouch, where she also kept her little clay figures bound with Edward's name in blood. "Afterwards, Father. Let's get to work, shall we? Time is of the essence."

The priest fumbled with the Holy Book, toothless mouth moving in a slurred prayer.

Edward stood across from Elizabeth, her hood now back, her hair falling out in long, shining coils as if she were not a widow about to wed a second time but a young, pure maiden, the May Queen of folklore. Jacquetta had twined spring flowers in her locks; a crown of Muguet de Bois, the Forget Me Not. Smiling, lost within her sensual, heavy-lidded eyes, the King took her hand and thought of the pleasures of the night ahead.

Outside, in the tangle of tree boughs, the old owl, eyes wide as golden lamps, hooted with renewed vehemence, as if wondering to witness these hidden nuptials. *Whooo Whooo* would dare wed in secret on old Beltaine Eve?

CHAPTER THIRTEEN

Weeks then a month passed at Grafton Woodville. Elizabeth Woodville sat disconsolately in the manor house, waiting to hear from Edward. No word came. Fractious and discomfited, she screeched at her sisters, wept at her mother's knee. "You told me I would have him! I did what you said but I was deceived in the end. Marriage or no, he still saw me as a whore and discarded me."

"There is still time," soothed Jacquetta. "Have patience, Bess."

Anthony Woodville, who had passed the doorway of his mother's solar and heard his sister's distressed cries, entered the room to the annoyance of both women, who railed at him.

"Elizabeth, stop!" He reached down and caught his sister's hands. They had always been close and it pained him to see her upset. "Do you think I do not know what went on May Day Eve? All the girls know too, we aren't fools. We know you went to St Mary and St Michael's Chapel with the King, and that when you came back, you took him to your chamber."

Elizabeth gaped at Anthony; usually calm and smooth, a thinker more than a fighter, he was almost trembling with what seemed to be ill-held rage. "You've proved yourself a fool, Elizabeth. You'll never hear from him again! He's had what he wanted…"

"But. We. Are. Married!" Elizabeth spat, tearing her hands out of her brother's in anger.

"And who witnessed it, except an old priest on death's door, mother and Edward's own page? Mother can hardly speak out on your behalf; she was a close companion of Queen Margaret—she's one of the enemy in Edward's eyes! We would be ruined if we dared to speak out! Ruined or worse! We have scarcely regained our positions in the world after the King and Queen were put to flight."

Agitated, he began to pace about the chamber. "There is more too, Bess; I don't know how to tell you."

"Just say it, Anthony!" she cried. "This is not the time to play games with me."

"There are rumours that he once took another wife—in secret—just like you."

"Rumours! I do not wish to hear rumours. Half of what men say are no more than idle lies."

"If he gulled you, sister, merely to get into your bed, what makes you think he might not have done so before."

Elizabeth's lip trembled but her eyes were sparkling with fury. Anthony fought the urge to cross himself; if the Woodville children were the descendants of the sorceress Melusine through Jacquetta, the tainted blood appeared to be coming out in Bess now. "Where is this other woman?" she snapped. "Does she yet live?"

"I do not know," he answered truthfully. "As I said, it is only a rumour. I just wanted you to have warning—that the King might never contact you again."

"Mother, mother, what shall I do? I cannot bear it," cried Elizabeth, tears starting as she whirled to face Jacquetta.

"My dear, we will think of something, I swear to you!" Jacquetta flapped her hand at her son. "Anthony, go, I beg you. You are making matters worse. I must speak to Elizabeth alone."

Anthony began to protest but his mother's icy glare quelled his tongue and he backed out of the chamber, slamming the door behind him.

"Calm yourself, Elizabeth." Jacquetta rose from her seat, taking a deep breath. "I have an idea. It is risky, but it might work."

"What?" Elizabeth wiped at her eyes.

Jacquetta eyed her daughter's lean figure. "You have had your courses since the King was here?"

Elizabeth nodded. "Yes, though I know not whether this is a good thing or bad."

"Pity," murmured Jacquetta. "Nonetheless, we will write to Edward and tell him you are pregnant. What every King wants is a bride who can bear him lots of healthy sons."

Elizabeth's hand flew to her mouth in shock. "Mother, I cannot tell such a lie to the King! When he finds out the truth…"

"You will tell him the child was lost—he can ask the physicians; they will surely inform him it is not an uncommon thing in early pregnancy, especially when the mother is…*distressed*. Distressed by the absence of her lawful, loving husband."

"What if he wants some kind of proof?"

Jacquetta's lips drew to bloodless lines. "Hopefully once he sees your sorrowing face, he will remember how beautiful you are and decide he wants to bed you yet again. If he does ask for more than your word, leave it to me—I will arrange something with the village midwife."

Elizabeth grimaced and then let out a long, bitter sigh. "I will do it. I want him, mother. Not just because he is King, although that brings its own attractions. I want him, now and always, for the rest of my natural life. I don't care if he seeks the bed of others, as long as he comes back to mine. *I want him!*"

"You will have him, Elizabeth." Jacquetta placed her hands on her daughter's shoulders. "I am sure of it. I prayed to St Joseph and St Anne, and then, I *saw* it come true within a waking dream—I saw you walk through the pillars of Westminster, I saw you pass the circle of dead kings, I saw you accept the crown and the Queen's sceptre." She took a deep breath. "I saw many children, girls and boys, and then…"

"Then what?" asked Elizabeth. She felt uncomfortable when her mother spoke of visions and dreams, but surely it was not wicked if Jacquetta had prayed to two Saints first?

"Then nothing. I don't know. It was dark, and I felt…I wanted to see no more."

A shiver ran up Elizabeth's spine but she fought back her unease, replacing it with a will of iron. Fear left her as she focused on her supreme desire. "I will be Queen," she murmured. "Edward will love me, and honour me, no matter what."

The house at East Hall, owned by the Duchess of Norfolk, was a beautiful place, Eleanor could not deny it. It was said to have roots back to the time of the Saxon kings, their long-gone timber palace lying beneath the present walls. As it stood now, East Hall was a proud flint building with a moat fed by a local spring. A long bridge crossed the deep moat and gave access to the battlemented gatehouse and internal courtyard with the usual kitchens, stables, chapel and hall blocks. It reminded her Blakemere, her childhood home, although it was much larger.

It was quieter than Blakemere, too, inhabited only by a small, discreet household provided by her sister Bet, and by Agnes who loyally had left her old life behind and followed her from Great Dorset. Such quietude as End Hall provided was good for the soul, though, and was ideal for reflecting on one's past sins and making atonement for them. A sense of peace had settled over now that she wore the brown scapular of the Carmelites and used the order's image on her seal ring. She no longer thought of Edward with longing; it was as if he was part of a strange, unsettling dream, an otherworldly prince who had walked from the mists and then retreated back into them. Now the only Prince she wished to serve was the Prince of Peace—Our Lord Jesus Christ.

Today though, Eleanor felt a hint of unease. Elizabeth was coming from Framlingham Castle to see her. While there was nothing unusual about that, the words in the letter Bet had sent were disturbing and mysterious. *Dear beloved sister, I will soon visit End Hall. I have much to tell you. Let us meet in the church, away from all others in the household. I bid you, do not even bring your maid, for there is business between us that must be done in private.*

Feeling suddenly exhausted, an unknown dread slowing her limbs, the young woman trudged down the rain-dampened path towards the church of St Mary. As it came into view, crouching in its green churchyard, she could see the Talbot hound on one high-flung buttress, barking up to heaven. She could not help but smile a little as she thought of Blanchette, old and arthritic, asleep in her basket back in East Hall. Entering the gloom of the church's nave through the south porch, she was greeted by the huge Rose En Soleil, Edward's symbol, in the eastern window, illuminated by stray rays of the weak sun. It was appropriate of course, the Mowbrays being good Yorkists, and Bet had placed it there to confirm their allegiance, but it unnerved Eleanor every time she saw it, reminding her of her folly and bygone shame.

Inside the church, she stood and waited. Behind her, the sun died and the White Rose wilted into shadow.

The door opened. Bet, still dressed in her riding attire, stepped over the threshold leaving her ladies and her guards waiting outside.

"Eleanor." The two sisters greeted with a light embrace.

"There is evil news…" Eleanor's voice was flat.

Elizabeth chewed her lip, twined her hands together. "I thought it best for you to know—the King is married."

Blood drained from Eleanor's cheeks. A long breath rushed between her lips. "I knew one day he would. There has been talk of a foreign princess. But I truly thought before it reached that point, he would seek me out to have our union annulled. As it is now, he…he has committed…

She could not get the word out.

"Bigamy," Elizabeth finished. "If ever anyone should find out what transpired between you and the King, any heirs of his body he might have could be accounted bastards."

Bile burnt Eleanor's mouth. "What…what a web of misfortune I may have wrought by cleaving to him!"

"It is not your fault, Nel!" Elizabeth admonished, clutching her sister's wrist. "It is the King's, none other."

"And who is the lucky bride?" A rueful smile twisted Eleanor's lips. "What foreign princess shall rule over us?"

Elizabeth shook her head. "No foreign princess. Listen, Nel, for this is the most scandalous tale of all. The French King wished for his queen's sister, Bona of Savoy, to marry Edward. Warwick pushed for the match, went to France to treat for Bona's hand. When he returned home, Edward openly scorned Bona and announced, out of the blue, that he was already married."

"He married an Englishwoman?"

"Yes. Elizabeth Grey, widow of the knight Sir John Grey. Daughter of Jacquetta Woodville, the former Duchess of Bedford. And…he married Dame Grey in secret on May Day Eve at her parents' manor at Grafton Woodville, keeping the marriage secret for over four months, until he was forced to reveal it by Warwick. The Earl is furious, as you might imagine."

"It…it was just like…" Eleanor stammered.

"Yes. Why he ultimately chose this Woodville woman over you, I do not know. However, that is what he has done. Soon he will proclaim her as his Queen in Reading Abbey."

Eleanor wiped a hand across her face; hot and cold waves flooded through her body. "What will this mean for me, do you think? Or has he forgotten my existence?"

"I doubt that, Nel." A shadow swept over Bet's face. "Up till now you were an inconvenience, an indiscretion born of his youthful folly. Now that he has wed Dame Grey—what you are and what you know is a threat. To his marriage, to the legitimacy of his children. To his Crown."

"Edward fought such bloody battles for the crown." Eleanor stared down at the floor. The sun had emerged from the clouds outside and a shaft of light burned through a saint's mantle in one of the painted glass windows; blood red light pooled on the flagstones of St Mary's. "He would stop anyone who tried to take it from him."

"Yes." Elizabeth clasped her sister's hand in her own. "Who knows what he would do to protect what he sees as his right?"

Eleanor made a little mewling sound of fear; her large, deep brown eyes became those of a hunted deer. "Bet, I am frightened."

"So am I," murmured her sister, "Maybe it will all come to nought and our fears be allayed in the end. But in the meantime, have great care in all you say and do."

Eleanor took a deep breath, battling her fear, her fingers stroking the sacred scapular she wore. "I am dedicated solely to God; I need not fear. I must put my trust in Him even more from now onwards. Whatever happens to me in the future is in His hands as part of His great plan. I must remain content with that."

CHAPTER FOURTEEN

Michaelmas Day. Beneath a stormy grey sky, Elizabeth Woodville walked imperiously through the Abbey complex at Reading. She wore a cloth of gold and her hair was tucked beneath a tall headdress. She held herself like a Queen—and sure enough, she would be proclaimed a Queen that day.

A little smile curved the pale bow of her lips. The ruse concocted with her mother, Jacquetta had worked God be praised. Edward had summoned her at once when hearing of a prospective child. When she reached him, she had fallen down prostrated in grief at his feet. The child had passed from her, she told him, through sobs; the midwife said it happened at least once to most women. There would be others—yes, he need only look at her mother's huge brood, and her sturdy, hale sons by John Grey, to know she would serve him well with children.

Although consumed by desperate disappointment at first, Edward had then sought to comfort her. Naturally, they had soon fallen into bed, and in his youth and ardour he had not seen, nor even bothered to ascertain, that there were no tell-tale signs of any recent pregnancy on her body. In the morning, he had arisen, full of determination. "Bess, God willing, you will never be separated from me again. Warwick bleats about a marriage with Bona of Savoy…"

Elizabeth's heart had flip-flopped at hearing her potential rival's name.

"But I have seen a painting of her and I like her not. Nor will I have Warwick dictate to me as if I were a feckless boy. I will have the Queen I want. You are my true-wedded wife, Elizabeth, and I swear you shall be my Queen."

And so he had told the lords that he had married in secret, and he weathered Warwick's storms as his kinsman shouted and flung about the chamber in a rage. "You will regret this mésalliance, Edward!"

Edward had boldly looked Warwick in the eye; quiet-spoken but with steel in his voice. "That I will not, Dick. Now get you gone from my sight, if all you can do is bray like an ass."

The announcement had taken place almost a month ago and now Elizabeth was here at Reading Abbey, on the Feast of Michaelmas, in the fading sunshine of late September, to be presented as Edward's Queen in the Abbey church of St Mary and St John the Evangelist. Her mother and sisters, Anne, Jacqui, Eleanor, Meg and Martha escorted her, but strutting before her like a preening pigeon was the King's oldest brother, George of Clarence.

Elizabeth eyed young George's back as he led her past the grand monastic buildings—the vestry, chapter house, monks' dormitory and infirmary—toward the magnificent Abbey church. Clarence was about fourteen with a halo of wild dark blond curls and a handsome enough countenance, but his expression was oftimes peevish and dissatisfied in a way she thought savoured of malice. She decided she did not like the boy, although he seemed pleased enough to have the honour of leading his new Queen into the Abbey. That, of course, was no doubt because it made him look important before the lords of the land, not that he bore any great love for his brother's new wife.

Well, if George was problematic, she'd soon see him cut down to size, now that she had the power. He was clearly puffed with pride since he was, at present, Edward's heir apparent. She'd soon end that when she bore Edward a son—and she had no doubt she would get with child soon. Ned was a man with strong carnal desires and she could provide what he wanted. She was glad at that moment that she was five years her husband's elder and not a shy, timorous virgin. She smiled to herself, the cat that stole the cream again. Yes, she would twist her husband around her finger in any way she could—and smug-faced George would find himself out in the cold. They'd have to find him a bride; maybe one of her sisters? So many girls; with a few blandishments, she hoped to find rich dukes and earls for them all. As for her two sons, Thomas and Richard, and her father and brothers—titles, she hoped. But that would come in time…

The little procession had reached the door of the Abbey Church. Richard Neville, Earl of Warwick appeared, clad in red robes and chaperon, to usher the party inside. The sight of his saturnine, sun-bronzed face glowering beneath his coiled dark hair made a nervous shudder run through her; she swiftly quelled it. A Queen must know no fear—and this day she would be a Queen.

Disdainfully she looked down the straight length of her nose at the Earl, while at the same time giving him a tight-lipped smile. He flushed even deeper under his tan and made a low but somewhat mocking bow. She ignored him.

This was her moment of all moments. She would let no one ruin it.

With grace and poise, she stepped over the threshold into the world of candlelight and shadows, of the mysteries of God. Vast painted pillars greeted her, and light spilt through a fair Rose Window. Passing down the ambulatory, she noted chantry chapels and shrines alight with a thousand tapers— one held, within a silver reliquary, the mummified arm of St James himself.

She had little time to marvel, though, as the Earl and George were striding on ahead in the direction of the high altar. Passing under the rood screen with its gaudy mass of carved saints, Elizabeth came into the presence of the great lords of England—and her husband, the King.

Edward stood in a cloak of ermine, a crown upon his brow, the majesty of his kingship giving him an almost otherworldly presence. Anointed and chosen by God.

And God had chosen Elizabeth too. For an instant, she nearly lost her composure, her eyes filling, but she blinked back the treacherous tears of joy and wonder. She could not weep, must not show unseemly emotion; she was beyond that, beyond the weaknesses of ordinary women.

At the head of the procession, Warwick and George halted. Elizabeth stood wreathed in light and candle-smoke, her tall headdress rising like a church spire through the heady vapours. She felt hostility from many of the men gathered in the choir—dour, war-hardened lords who were shocked at Edward's choice of a bride who was dowry-less, older than the King, and the mother of two children. Yet she sensed admiration, too, the legacy of the great beauty which charmed so many men. She knew many of them had spoken ill of her and even encouraged the King to annul the match, but Ned refused and the lords were silent and obedient now.

They would have to be. She, Elizabeth, was their Queen.

Edward stepped forward and proffered his hand. Head bowed modestly, she took it. Her fingers did not tremble, not even a little.

"Lords of England, look upon your Queen!" It was Warwick who shouted aloud, the words sounding strangled in his throat. He drew his sword and raised it in salute as did young George, his face shining in the candlelight—like a pretty imp, Elizabeth thought.

The great and mighty of England, the Mowbrays, Lord Faulconberg, the Nevilles, John Howard, William Herbert, the de la Poles, the Bourchiers, the Fitz Alans and others began bowing and calling out in acclamation of their new Queen. Anthony stood amongst them, as handsome as Sir Lancelot—the Woodville family had been pardoned for their earlier Lancastrian affiliation, and Anthony, having become Lord Scales in right of his wife, was set to have new honours and positions given to him. He beamed at Elizabeth, full of brotherly pride; Anthony, who had once chided her for cleaving to Edward's will, who thought the King had deserted her.

Her brother's pessimism was proven wrong—and she was now proclaimed Queen. Elizabeth, Queen Consort of Edward IV.

Edward and Elizabeth stayed at Reading Abbey for two weeks after Elizabeth's presentation to the lords. They strolled through the streets of the town with great ceremony, and the townsfolk greeted them with celebration, showering the couple with Michaelmas daisies and performing pageants and plays. They visited Abbey properties beyond the walls of the religious compound such as the mill by Holy Brook, and rode to the nearby shrine of Our Lady of Caversham to kneel in prayer. Edward heard pleas from the master of the leper hospital, who complained that the Abbot, John Thorn, had kept the hospital's monies for himself. Elizabeth did not involve herself with such ugliness, of course, but worked on making herself as fair, sweet and pliable as she could, to keep Edward's eyes upon her and charm the local populace. She showed her piety to the monks and Abbot Thorn by attending masses dawn to dusk, kissing the withered hand of blessed St James and offering prayers for the soul of Edward's ancestor, King Henry I, who lay in a vast tomb near the High Altar of Reading Abbey.

Growing weary of so much prayer and kneeling, at length she retired to her chamber and summoned her mother to her side. Together they drank hippocras and ate wafers and candied violets that sweetened the breath.

"Well, mother, all is well. Edward is mine. All I ask of you now is to give me some of your potions to conceive a son. That is what I need to bind my lord to me for all time. To make him love me forever. A son."

"I would not endanger you with such elixirs, my sweeting," said Jacquetta. "The King has shared your bed every night and stays till dawn; I am sure he will put a child in your belly soon."

"How do you know such things about my private hours with Ned?" Elizabeth's cheeks turned rosy. "You are staying in the Abbey Hospitium with my sisters."

"Ah, I have ears, daughter. People talk and all the monks blush whenever you and his Grace walk by. I believe they have to sing louder at chapel in the morn…"

"Mother!" gasped Elizabeth, mortified. "I do not want to hear this! I am the Queen."

"You are indeed. And soon, I trow, you will be the mother of a prince."

Just at that moment, Edward walked in, stopping with hands on hips and leaving his courtiers to disperse in the corridors beyond. He looked a little startled to see Jacquetta with her daughter and perhaps somewhat irritated. The former Duchess of Bedford curtseyed and made her excuses to leave.

"Did you assuage the lepers?" Elizabeth asked, feigning interest. She was glad she had not had to stand anywhere near the sufferers of that horrid affliction, with their rotted noses, corpse-like bandages and ringing bells.

"Oh, yes. Whether Thorn was holding back the coin or not, I cannot say, but he blustered and had a chest of money brought over right away and promised the hospital would have the repairs to the roof. But enough of that talk, come walk with me."

Together they strolled through the Abbey's magnificent cloister where the capitals of the Romanesque arches were adorned by primaeval carved monsters and bug-eyed birds with pointed beaks, among more standard religious carvings such as the Coronation of the Virgin Mary.

Beneath the stone depicting the Virgin with Christ placing a crown upon His Mother's head, Edward paused. He glanced around; all the monks had scuttled away to give the royal couple privacy. His usual smile was gone, his brow uncharacteristically creased.

Elizabeth shifted uncomfortably in her thin jewelled slippers. The day seemed to have grown darker, colder. "My lord husband, you look troubled as I have never seen you before. What ails you?" She placed a reassuring hand on his arm.

"I…I *am* troubled. There is something I must tell you. Do not hate me, Bess."

A chill bit at her innards, turning her blood to ice. She felt her heartbeat thudding in her own ears and struggled to keep her composure. Surely, surely, he could not put her aside now—but maybe that accursed Warwick had dripped poison in his ear and convinced him of the desirability of Bona of Savoy.

"Edward, my *husband*," she stressed the word, "you are frightening me. What is wrong? I beg you speak."

The King leaned back against a pillar; the grotesque carved on its capital leered and jerked the corners of its wide mouth with its fingers as if mocking the man below. "When I was flush with victory, with Mortimer's Cross behind me, I was travelling through the country toward London…" he began in a low voice.

Elizabeth's wild heartbeat began to subside. So, not about Bona, then. Whatever it was he was about to divulge, she could face it.

"I met a woman there…"

I don't want to hear about your other women, she thought angrily but kept her peace, not wishing to seem shrewish.

"I believed I was in love with her…for a time."

Elizabeth suddenly smiled. "I know what this confession is about. Elizabeth Wayte, and her son, little Arthur. *Your* son. I know about her already, my lord husband; such news is hard to keep quiet. It is nothing. What King has not a few bastards somewhere?"

Edward let out an audible groan and thumped the pillar with his curled fist in frustration. "It is not about Elizabeth Wayte."

"Who then?" Her voice rose; swiftly, she moderated it.

"Eleanor…Eleanor, daughter of the old Earl of Shrewsbury."

The name meant little to her. She knew the Duchess of Norfolk was a daughter of the late Earl but she knew nothing of another sister. She did not understand why Edward seemed so upset about this other woman. A pang of jealousy needled her—and the fear was back, descending in a black cloud. She had no idea why he was reluctant to speak of this woman; she had already told him that she knew of his indiscretions and did not care.

"Edward." Her voice shook. "What is this Eleanor to you?"

The King grimaced; his visage suddenly took on a guilty aspect. "Elizabeth..." His huge hand reached out to clamp on her wrist, drawing her close. "I was an enamoured fool; I made a terrible mistake. I...I married Eleanor in secret at her manor of Great Dorset."

Blood rushed to Elizabeth's head; the world spun around her. Edward clutched her to his chest, keeping her from striking the hard flagstones of the cloister floor.

"Elizabeth...Bess, listen to me!"

"What have you done?" she cried, careless of her tongue. "What possessed you to marry me when you were already..."

His palm descended over her mouth, silencing her. "Be still...still, my love. I was foolish but be not afraid, she will not harm us now."

"Is she dead?" spat Elizabeth, full of bitterness.

"Almost as good as. She has become a tertiary of the Carmelites."

"Tertiaries can be married."

"True, but I have had word she is married only to God and has put the past behind her. She has never tried to contact me or bring me any embarrassment."

"What about an annulment? Can you not have the marriage ended legally?"

"I think it would only complicate the matter, Bess. Bring it into the open where it would be used against me...*us*. It is better if it is kept secret forever."

"Are you sure she will never tell?"

"As sure as I can be."

"But as long as she lives, a chance will remain that she will reveal the truth."

"Yes."

They stood together in silence as beyond the cloister the sky grew suddenly black and a thin, grey drizzle began to fall.

CHAPTER FIFTEEN

Ice-frosted leaves crunching beneath her feet, Eleanor walked through the winter-hardened grounds of East Hall with her sister Elizabeth. The Duchess was clad in a grey, furred cloak; Eleanor still wore the scapular of the Carmelites with only a few under layers to protect her against the bite of the wintry weather. On the nearby fishponds, a thin veneer of ice glistened in the wan sun.

"Should you be so flimsily clad?" asked Bet with a frown, eyeing her sister's rather unsuitable attire. "It is winter or hadn't you noticed?"

"I am fine, do not fuss," said Eleanor, with a wry little smile. "God will shield me."

Elizabeth gazed thoughtfully at her sibling, trying to hide the concern she felt. Nel had become far more unworldly in the last few years, ever since the King married Elizabeth Woodville. She had taken religion to her heart, which was not in itself an evil thing, but she feared Eleanor had ceased to care for the necessities of daily life, growing almost ascetic as her religious fervour increased. She did not look well, shadows hung under her eyes and her cheekbones were sharp as blades. The dark eyes that had once shone with rich, jewel-like intensity had grown dull, lifeless.

"I wish you would come to Framlingham," Bet said, as she had many times in the past. "I would feel happier with you at my side."

"I am happy here with Agnes...and God. I would not wish to become involved in any kind of courtly life again."

Bet took a deep breath. "I will speak plainly to you, Nel. You look unwell. I would have you see a physician."

Eleanor turned her face away. "It has been a hard year...our mother Margaret, dead. I still grieve."

"So do I," said Elizabeth, crossing herself, "and I always will, but there are three children, the children of our late brother, Viscount Lisle, who were in her care. We are their guardians now and should be strong for them."

"Oh yes…" Eleanor sounded as if she had forgotten there were children jointly in her guardianship. "What were their names again? Margaret, Elizabeth and what was the other? John?"

"Thomas, Nel. After our brother," said Elizabeth softly. How could Nel have forgotten?

"You must be the one to care for them; in my position, I truly cannot," Eleanor suddenly said, as a harsh cough wracked her body.

"I knew you needed a warmer cloak," chided Bet. "You will catch your death."

"And wouldn't some be pleased by that?" said Eleanor with a bitter laugh.

"Eleanor, perhaps we were wrong. Three years have passed."

"No." The dark eyes turned midnight in the white face. "*They* watch, you know. There are strangers in Kenninghall. A few have even worked at the Hall. I know they are sent from him."

"Why did you let strangers in, if you thought such things? I would have sent you more servants if you needed them. Trusted folk from my own household."

"I wanted them to take back news to Edward that I am content with my lot and would never try to take jealous revenge."

Elizabeth began to pace. "I would rather not say this, but it must be said—it may not be Edward you need fear most. It is the jealousy and suspicion of another that might be your problem."

"The Queen?" Eleanor looked startled. "Do you think he told her?"

"He may well have; who can say what was in his mind? I can tell you now, she is a proud and jealous woman, for all that she shares him with his harlots. Did you hear about the death of Thomas Fitzgerald in Ireland?"

Eleanor shook her head, looking shocked. "I did not know Fitzgerald was dead. Was he not one of the King's riding companions?"

"Yes, they were friends but, in his cups, Fitzgerald dared jest about Elizabeth's birth and former marriage, and called her the King's Grey Mare."

Eleanor let out a gasp and pressed a hand to her mouth. Lowering it, she breathed, "And what did Edward do then?"

"Edward? Nothing. He laughed and took it as a jest rather than an insult! Both men clapped each other on the shoulder afterwards, and Edward merely scolded Fitzgerald for his loose tongue. However, tales of Fitzgerald's jibes soon got back to the Queen, and it was said her wrath was terrible…" Elizabeth licked her lips. "A few weeks ago, John Tiptoft executed Fitzgerald for treason. A rumour has sprung up that two of his children were murdered at the same time—two young boys who had been at their lessons."

"And you think she…"

"The King was said to be grieved at the news of Fitzgerald's death. Grieved. And yet no one has been taken to task for the execution. If the King did not put his seal to the death warrant, who did?"

"It…it must be a mistake. I cannot imagine."

"I am not so sure. I attended Elizabeth's coronation, and you would have thought no person more regal had ever trod the tiles of Westminster, for all that her father was a mere knight! At the banquet, even her own mother was made to kneel at her feet in silence, moving only when Elizabeth signalled to her. She did the same to Edward's sister, the Lady Margaret; although she is Queen and may order such things, it is not protocol and need not have taken place. More than a few eyebrows were raised, especially with Margaret, who is the King's own blood."

Eleanor wrapped her arms around herself; the air seemed even colder; the north wind hissed over the dried-out grasses on the earthworks of East Hall. "Well, she need not fear. Edward's transgressions do not reflect on her. I bear her no ill will."

"I do not think that would matter to the Queen. Still she would see you as a threat, especially since she has not yet produced a male child. The Princess Elizabeth is a beautiful babe, no doubt about it, but she is…a girl."

The wind rose again, tossing ice crystals out of the grey sky into the women's faces. Spring was very late this year and showed no signs of making its welcome return

"Let us go to the house and sit before the fire." Bet placed her hand on her sister's arm. "It is not good to think on these matters too much."

Eleanor was unwell. At night she slept seldom and sweated often, tossing and turning on soaked sheets. Agnes would tend her, clucking over her thin, almost frail body. But then a messenger came from Great Dorset telling Agnes that her old mother was sick and like to die—she was a great age, nearly eighty summers—and that she was begging to see her daughter one last time. So with many a tear, Agnes had gone to attend to sorrowful family duties, leaving Eleanor with a heap of possets and tinctures the maid had brewed herself.

Eleanor had never felt so alone in the great old manor house with its creaking roof and high walls painted a dull red. She wanted to see Elizabeth but her sister was preparing for a great journey—she was to accompany Margaret Plantagenet, Edward's sister, to Burgundy, where she would marry its Duke, Charles the Bold. Eleanor felt so weak of limb she dared not travel far beyond the village, not even to the Carmel in Norwich, where she surmised at least her peace of mind would be greater than at East Hall.

"You need to be bled, I reckon, Lady," mumbled Thomasin, an old woman from the village who had come to attend Eleanor in Agnes' absence. She stopped folding her mistress' garments and took a step towards the door. "Should I call the barber?"

"No, Thomasin, not, not yet." Eleanor shuddered at the thought of the bawling barber of Kenninghall coming anywhere near her with his lancet and bleed-bowl. He was a hairless, pig-featured man who was drunk half the time and never washed his blood-stained apron; his cures were worse than most illnesses.

She felt the serving woman's rheumy, disapproving eyes follow her as she pulled her stool over nearer to the brazier in the solar. The big old House seemed colder and less friendly than when she had first arrived from Great Dorset. Her bones ached, her chest hurt with each breath; she was a young woman still but felt aged, as if a wizard's wand had touched her, casting an evil spell to rob her of her beauty and vitality.

"You should be in bed, mistress," muttered Thomasin, her whiskery chin bobbing, "and, I dare say it, bled."

Eleanor made to protest again, but suddenly there was a noisy clatter in the hall below, a banging door, the thud of feet on the tiles. Blanchette the hound, ever loyal though old and arthritic, leapt out of her cushioned basket near the fire and began to bark with fury.

"Hush, dog!" Eleanor spoke firmly to the hound and went towards the chamber door.

The steward, a burly fellow who had only taken the position a month or two back after the old steward died, huffed up the short flight of stairs from the lower level, his face the purplish hue of a plum.

"What is all that racket, Rogier?" asked Eleanor with some irritation. "Is anything amiss?"

"Messenger at the gate, milady—I let him in."

"You let…Who is he?" Nervous butterflies whirled in her belly. Pray God nothing had happened to Elizabeth or any of her other kin. Or…

"I don't know, milady."

Eleanor stared at the nearby slit of the window; beyond the glass, dusk had fallen, shrouding the earthwork and the village beyond. "It's after dark, yet you let him in. You let him in and did not find out from whence he came."

The man flushed but there was defiance in his stance too, which unnerved Eleanor. At one time, no man of Rogier's status would have spoken to her so. "He is wearing fine garb and has a good horse; I don't think he's out for robbing us."

"Just as well," said Eleanor, staring the man down, "since he is already within my house. I will go and meet with him."

She pushed past the steward and entered the Great Hall. It was dark, with only a few candelabras casting a warm, hazy glow. The gloom-blurred faces of wooden angels smiled down from the roofbeams.

A man was standing by the fireplace, which had recently been installed by Elizabeth; it had a marble mantlepiece and supporting pillars carved with Talbot hounds. The man wore a dark woollen cloak and leather boots which looked quite new. He was young, arrogant of mien, and unsmiling as Eleanor approached. No badge or other device was attached to his garments. That was ominous.

He stood gazed at Eleanor for a moment and she halted in her tracks, with no greeting. After a moment, he bowed in what seemed to her a grudging manner.

She brought forth all the courtesy she could muster, learnt at her mother's knee. "Give me your name, sir, and your business, and when all is said, you may partake of wine or ale, as you wish, brought to you by my steward, Rogier."

The man cleared his throat. "I am but a humble messenger, my name would mean nought. You are Eleanor Boteler, widow of Thomas?"

"I am," she said, and a little angry fire kindled in her heart, "but I am much more than the widow of a knight. And you may know me by the name by which I was born. Talbot. The name of my father, the Earl of Shrewsbury."

"My apologies, my Lady." Another curt bow. "I did not mean to offend."

"Why are you here, whoever you may be? Who sent you?"

The man cleared his throat and his gaze swivelled over to Rogier the Steward. "I have a missive for you, my Lady. That is all." Reaching under his cloak, he drew out a parchment with blue wax sealing it. The shape of the seal has been smudged into illegibility. Brusquely he handed it to Eleanor and then turned swiftly on his heel as if to leave.

"Wait!" she said, clutching the scroll. "Do you not want to rest, to refresh yourself? I will pay you for your trouble."

"No need, Dame Boteler," he said, putting the emphasis on her married name, and then he was gone, his boots clattering in the hallways, leaving her astounded at his rudeness.

Rogier was lurking around the Hall, a rotund figure in the shadows. "You..." she turned on him, eyes flashing, "get out. See that our 'guest' leaves the manor without delay—and that the gate is barred behind him. No one, you hear me, man, no one is to come onto this property without my prior say so."

Rogier swallowed, his Adam's apple bobbing, and then he fled from the Great Hall. The main door of the house banged; in the distance, a horse's hooves could be heard growing fainter and fainter, until, at last, blessed silence reigned.

Eleanor lit a few more candles, giving herself extra light. Sitting in a window embrasure below the smiling angels, she opened the letter. She did not recognise the hand it was written in but she had not expected to; no doubt, a scribe or some minion had written it. The words were few and there was, naturally, no signature on the bottom: *I trust your continued discretion about past matters, Dame Boteler. Do not fail, on the fear of the greatest of displeasures. Silence is your gain and in religious piety your safety.*

Eleanor felt a flood of anger and crushed the parchment in her hands. "It's a threat!!" she cried out to the dust motes, the carven angels with their serene countenances. "A bloody threat!"

And then she burst into tears, which fell upon the crumpled letter and blurred the ink to blobs of darkness

The months dragged on. Eleanor barely ate, seldom left the safety of East Hall. She used her *prie dieu* for prayer as much as she used the chapel. Even when summer sun blasted the earth with heated breath, she remained locked in the dim dark house, on her knees, casting her gaze towards heaven.

And then one day she could not rise from the *prie dieu*; her knees buckled and she fell heavily on the floor and could not get up again. Her countenance was ashen, her dark eyes glittering with fever.

The old woman Thomasin scurried to her side, pulling her upright. "I am putting you to bed, mistress," she said firmly, "and calling in the barber surgeon to bleed you. I won't hear otherwise."

Eleanor protested but was too weak to have much fight in her. She lay like a shrivelled leaf in the centre of her canopied bed. She'd brought it in pieces from Great Dorset when she left Warwickshire; it was the bed she had shared with King Edward for such a brief time. Lying there, eyes half- closed, she almost fancied she could smell him on the sheets—an idle fancy for they were sheets given her by Bet as a gift. Nonetheless, she thought she could discern his scent; masculine smells of leather tinged by clean sweat and the frankincense and sandalwood he wore.

The horrible butcher of a barber surgeon arrived, an apprentice boy in tow; she heard him mount the stair, blustering away in a voice that boomed throughout the hall, talking to Thomasin of tooth-plucking and fixing old men's piles. "Well, my Lady," he said to Eleanor as he entered the chamber (at the very least, he had removed his blood-spattered apron), "I will soon have you on your feet again. You clearly have an overabundance of bad blood and hence your humours have gone awry. You will not recover until they have been balanced."

"I do not wish to be bled," said Eleanor faintly.

"Now, now, it shan't take long. I have my sharpest lancet ready." He beckoned to his assistant, a pimply-faced lad who brought over the barber's tools of the trade and a bowl. He looked sweaty and eager.

"Thomasin," Eleanor struggled to rise, "I told you…"

"Everyone's affeared for your health, mistress," said the old woman shrilly. "You don't know what you're sayin'. It's all for the best; it's what is needed."

Eleanor shook her head but the barber was looming over her, drink-breathed and over-jolly. "It shan't take long, shan't take long at all."

The lancet bit deep; the blood flowed, glistening like rich red wine into the bowl. The young apprentice looked at it so greedily, Eleanor thought he was half of a mind to drink it.

Old Thomasin was laving her hot forehead all the while. "You'll feel better soon, my Lady. So much better."

"Just leave me," Eleanor murmured, turning her face to the wall.

Despite the bleeding, she did not improve. Food she refused, taking no more than a few sips of broth that tasted foul as poison in her mouth. She lay abed, holding an alabaster carving of the Virgin in her arms; it had come from Nottingham long ago and had belonged to her mother. It gave her some small comfort as she dreamed of better days long ago. Old Blanchette, leaving her basket, lay on the coverlet of her bed, head down, eyes big and sorrowful.

One morning Eleanor woke up…and could not feel her legs. "Thomasin!" she screamed for the servant, "quickly, I bid you, send to Great Dorset for Agnes. I want her to return at once if she would. And then…summon my lawyers in all haste. I…I must needs make my will."

The lawyers arrived, darkly dressed men in tall large hats resembling chimney stacks. When they were all gathered in attendance, a murder of crows hovering around her bedside, Eleanor dictated her last will and testament to them, leaving all of her lands and properties to Elizabeth, including a reversion on the ones Edward had given her. She made provisions to her servants, especially Agnes, and confirmed that her place of burial would be in the House of the Carmelites in Norwich.

Hearing of her illness, Elizabeth rode in with her own physician but Eleanor waved him away. "I know my own end," she said, "and I accept it. At night I see the glory of God within my mind, and all fear leaves me. I no longer require food, drink or any earthly thing. I desire only to dwell in the halls of Our Father unto eternity…"

Elizabeth wept. "I feel I should stay here and nurse you, Nel, but soon, soon I must go over the sea with the Lady Margaret. Perhaps I could ask the King to release me from my duties to his sister."

"No, Bet; you must not. You must do your duty to Ned and the House of York, even as I do mine towards God." Weakly, she crossed herself; her cheeks were like those of the alabaster statue she bore in the crook of her arm; her face was that of an ascetic, a mystic, peaceful, half in another realm. Light streaming from the shutters glowed through her near-translucent skin, highlighting the veins, blue and fine at her temples. Outside, in the village, children played on the green, their eager voices carried to East Hall on the summer wind, but it was, on this day, an strangely melancholy sound—a sound of the world of the living.

A world Eleanor was leaving.

"Eleanor, I beg you, hold fast for me until I return from Burgundy," Elizabeth implored, tears trailing down her cheeks. "This cannot be, you are young yet; you can get better."

"I have no will to get better," murmured Eleanor. "I wish for nothing more than to see the glory of Christ—but, I love you, my sister, and I will try to wait for you. But if I cannot, do not mourn, for be assured, our parting will not be eternal."

Elizabeth continued to weep as she rose from her sister's bedside. She took one long, lingering look at the small, still shape upon the pillows of the great bed, and then she left Kenninghall and did not look back. Red-eyed and silent in her grief, she fared to Framlingham alone in her litter, taking no comfort from any upon the journey home.

Eleanor died upon the 30th day of June, a hot day with a bright sun hanging like a coin in the sky, with only Agnes, newly ridden in from Dorset, to weep for her. Elizabeth was far away, at the court of the Duke of Burgundy, where the courtiers of the Burgundian Court called her 'the most beautiful woman in England.' But if she was the fairest, she was also the most melancholy, heavy with grief, forcing a smile to her lips as the tall Margaret of York, made even more statuesque by her towering conical headdress, stooped to kiss the lips of her short, stocky husband during the celebrations.

By the time Elizabeth had returned from the festivities surrounding the marriage, Eleanor had been laid to rest within the friary church of the Carmelites as she had wished. In her last days, she had outlined plans for a simple chest tomb, without effigy and decorated with weepers based on members of her family. Elizabeth would see it wrought to her memory.

Elizabeth was minded to visit the priory to pray for her sister's soul and pay the friars to do likewise in perpetuity, but she found she was unable to go, for other matters pressed, disturbing and unexpected. Much to her shock and dismay, two of her seemingly loyal servants were arrested on the King's orders as Lancastrian sympathisers working for the

Duke of Somerset—tried for treason, they were hastily executed at Tower Hill.

She was sure her men were innocent; they had accompanied her abroad and had shown no signs of their supposed perfidy. But who was she to argue, especially with Edward? She had no strength left to question; Eleanor was dead, and that sorrow preyed upon her night and day—she should have left more attendants to care for her sister, to watch over her.

And her troubles soon escalated. The King's anger descended upon Elizabeth when it came to his attention that Eleanor had bequeathed all her lands to the Duchess. *No licence has been granted for the conveyance of these properties*, Edward raged, and he promptly confiscated them all, even Griff, which Eleanor had returned to Lord Sudeley not long after she was first widowed and he had no real right to take, save that he was King and he could. Elizabeth heard that old Lord Sudeley, Eleanor's former father-in-law, also felt the heavy hand of Edward; without warning, Edward stripped Boteler of his favourite castle and gave it to his youngest brother, Richard, a youth of only sixteen.

In Framlingham, behind the high curtain walls of the fortress, Elizabeth thought of all these recent events and was distressed. She was Duchess of Norfolk and even she was afraid; she feared too that the King's ire over the matter of the lands might affect her marriage to John, who as the King's kinsman, sought ever to rise in his favour.

She sighed a deep breath of relief when news reached her that Edward, his harshness abating, had decided to grant her a full pardon 'for all offences.'

She could continue her life as best she could.

But she would never forget Eleanor...and her secret.

The little blond girl danced through the herb garden, her hair a halo of golden curls about her smiling face. Happily, she chased blue-winged and white-winged butterflies amidst the herbs and flowers—rue, rosemary, sage and thyme.

At the far end of the garden, Edward King of England stood with Queen Elizabeth, watching as their little daughter, Elizabeth of York, ran and played, chased by her white-wimpled nurses.

Elizabeth smiled and nodded. "She is a healthy, beautiful child, is she not?"

"That she is," said Edward, but his gaze was focussed elsewhere—as if he saw not the child, nor even the garden.

His distractedness always bothered Elizabeth; she assumed it came when he was thinking of other women. She knew they existed, of course, for Edward was a lusty man, but she did not want her husband to muse on them when he was spending time with her.

"Our newest daughter, Mary, shall be equally fair, I deem," she said, trying to draw his attention back to where it belonged. "We will have a large family, just as my parents did—and yours, my dearest husband."

Edward cast her a smile that seemed a little forced.

Elizabeth tried again. "And the babe I carry now beneath my belt—I am sure it will be your son and heir this time."

Elizabeth had Edward's attention now. He turned to her, face solemn. "Yes, we need an heir to my throne. A legitimate heir."

She hated the way he emphasised 'legitimate'. She knew what he had done and that her knowledge of his bigamy meant they could never be legally married, even though Eleanor Talbot was now dead and rotting in Whitefriars. At least there was no longer a chance she could ever speak out, and hopefully Ned had cowed that silly sister of hers into eternal silence, the one who shared Elizabeth's name and was, the Queen thought uncharitably, often wrongfully called 'the most beautiful English lady', a title that surely should be reserved for England's Queen…

"When he is born, his position will be safe now, will it not?" she asked in a whisper, seeking assurance. It was not often Elizabeth Woodville needed assurance, but on this terrible, secret matter she most surely did.

"Ah, so serious, Bess!" Edward's eyes warmed and he slipped his arm around her waist. "Of course, his position will be safe. Who could bring us harm?"

Overhead, a cloud slipped over the sun, plunging the garden into sudden gloom. Little Elizabeth ceased her playing and glanced up as if in surprise.

"What about the priest...that...that Stillington?" Elizabeth's voice was harsh, losing its usual sultry timbre.

"I have made him a Bishop, even when the Pope preferred another," said Edward cheerfully. "He will hold his tongue. He knows what is best for him."

"I hope you are right, husband," murmured Elizabeth, cradling the slight swell of her belly beneath its covering of silver-grey silk.

Overhead, the cloud dispersed, blown away on a fresh wind; the sun shone out again, golden, the Sunne in Splendour. Little Elizabeth of York lifted her chubby arms towards its brightness and her laughter was fairy bells across the royal garden.

AUTHORS NOTES:

Eleanor Talbot is a controversial figure. It was her alleged pre-contract to Edward IV that nullified his marriage, and her children's inheritance, allowing Richard of Gloucester to assume the throne. Many over the years thought she was an invention, and certain writers such as Thomas More confused her (deliberately?) with other of Edward IV's conquests such as Elizabeth Lucy (Wayte.) Even recently I saw someone on a website saying, 'Ricardians claim that she was the daughter of the Earl of Shrewsbury' as if that might not be the case. Ricardians don't 'claim' this; it was written right in Titulus Regius, and certainly John Talbot had a daughter Eleanor who took religious vows and was buried at Whitefriars in Norwich, the House of the Carmelites. A few arches and walls of this monastic house remain, and the magnificently carved portal doorway is preserved in Norwich today, although not in situ.

What many people don't realise about Eleanor Talbot is how well-connected she was. She wasn't just some simple girl Edward met. Her father had been a war hero. She was a niece of Warwick, so cousin to Isabel and Anne Neville. Her sister Elizabeth was the Duchess of Norfolk—and attended Richard's coronation, which seems hardly likely if he was somehow maligning her dead sister, to whom she appears to have been close.

People ask 'Well, why didn't the Talbot family pipe up during Edward's reign?' Shakespeare makes Edward look like a stolid old duffer who let everything untoward go on about him and was rather harmless and ineffective. Nothing was further from the truth. To cross Edward was never a wise thing to do, and the main family members at this time were women. As it happened, Eleanor, aged just 32, died when her sister Elizabeth was out of the country, and upon her return several of her servants were arrested and executed for treason, the circumstances of which are not really known. Edward also was furious that Eleanor had passed her lands, including the mysterious Wiltshire properties that she was unlikely to have ever have afforded to buy herself, to her sister without licence—and promptly confiscated them all.

I think Edward DID marry Eleanor in young, foolish lust. Bishop Stillington's strange spell of imprisonment (with no reason known) points towards it, as does some of George of Clarence's behaviour. Certainly, there were rumours about the validity of Edward's marriage BEFORE Richard ever claimed the throne as mentioned by Mancini.

After all, think about it—Edward married Elizabeth, a pretty Lancastrian widow several years old than himself, in secret, and kept the marriage under wraps for four months until he was being pressured about a marriage alliance with Bona of Savoy.

This is almost identical to what he did with Eleanor, except that he never acknowledged her for reasons unknown, perhaps because he quite simply was under no pressure to. The ways of the heart can be fickle after all. Maybe he actually fell in love with Elizabeth while he was just 'in lust' with Eleanor, maybe he thought her more likely to produce an heir since Eleanor had no children and Elizabeth had two when they met, or maybe he even just felt so pressured over

Bona that he stuck to his guns and said he was doing things his way. (After all, look at his grandson, Henry VIII, who did just that…)

Does anyone *truly* think Edward IV WOULDN'T have done it?

There is only one non-fiction book that really deals with Eleanor's life and attempts to reconstruct her time with Edward and the aftermath of their liaison, and that is THE SECRET QUEEN by the late John Ashdown-Hill. I thoroughly recommend it, for all those interested in learning more about this forgotten lady.

Other Notes-All songs/poems are my translations of medieval originals.

GREAT DORSET was the medieval name of the village we call BURTON DASSETT today. The church exists—and Edward IV did indeed, for some reason, send money for its upkeep…

Grafton Woodville exists and is known as Grafton Regis today. There is a church with a Woodville monument inside but the site of the 'secret wedding' was probably over the way in the Hermitage where excavations found a series of tiles with both Woodville and Yorkist symbols, which were probably added later to commemorate the event.

IF YOU HAVE ENJOYED THIS STORY, PLEASE CHECK OUT MY OTHER BOOKS:

Medieval Women—

MY FAIR LADY—ELEANOR OF PROVENCE, HENRY III'S LOST QUEEN

MISTRESS OF THE MAZE—THE LEGEND OF ROSAMUND CLIFFORD (Henry II's famous mistress.)

THE CAPTIVE PRINCESS—Eleanor of Brittany, who spent most of her life imprisoned and whose brother was the tragic Arthur of Brittany.

THE WHITE ROSE RENT—Richard III's illegitimate daughter, Katherine.

Richard III and the Wars of the Roses-

I, RICHARD PLANTAGENET-TANTE LE DESIREE-First person novel about Richard as Duke of Gloucester.

I RICHARD PLANTAGENET-LOYAULTE ME LIE—First person novel of Richard as King.

I, RICHARD PLANTAGENET COMPLETE. All in one volume containing TANTE LE DESIREE and LOYAULTE ME LIE

SACRED KING-Historical fantasy about Richard in the afterlife and his return to the world in a Leicester carpark.

WHITE ROSES, GOLDEN SUNNES—Collection of short stories about Richard III and his family.

A MAN WHO WOULD BE KING—A novel about Richard friend/enemy, Henry Stafford, Duke of Buckingham, told from Buckingham's first-person perspective.

BLOOD OF ROSES—Edward IV's victories at Mortimer's Cross and Towton.

STONEHENGE:

THE STONEHENGE SAGA COMPLETE. All in one edition of 2 earlier novels STONE LORD and MOON LORD. Ritual, war and death in early Bronze Age Britain—with an Arthurian twist!

ROBIN HOOD:

THE HOOD GAME: RISE OF THE GREENWOOD KING. Historical fantasy with a young peasant called Robyn winning the Hood in an ancient rite and assuming the mantle of the Greenwood King.

THE HOOD GAME: SHADOW OF THE BRAZEN HEAD. Guy of Gisburne is dead—but the Sheriff hires a necromancer to bring about his return!

OTHER:

A DANCE THROUGH TIME. Timeslip romantic fantasy. A London photographer falls through the stage in an old theatre and into Victorian times.

MY NAME IS NOT MIDNIGHT. Dystopian fantasy. Esmerelda lives in the world of winter, controlled by the religious group known as the Sestren.

19552665R00121

Printed in Great Britain
by Amazon